"Does That Blush Go All Over, Honey?"

Joey's grin was too conceited for words. "Let me see."

He yanked at Heather's blanket, but gently, just to tease her. She held on ferociously.

"You're in a different mood this morning, my pet," he said.

"I'm not...your pet...."

"Last night you were most...affectionate. You couldn't get enough of me. You were...*we* were...well, pretty incredible."

Her gut twisted in fresh shame. "I don't believe you."

"Fine. Suit yourself." He chuckled, but her words had wiped that tender eagerness from his gaze. "Your head hurts, I'll bet. You probably don't remember much.... Lucky for you, I remember everything. So, if you get curious, I could describe our night together in the most vivid detail. In fact, I'd love to do so."

She clamped her hands over her ears. "I'm living in a nightmare.... How could you sink so low as to seduce me?"

"You have it all backwards. *You* seduced me. For your information, I put up one hell of a fight defending my...er...virtue."

Dear Reader,

This May we invite you to delve into six delicious new titles from Silhouette Desire!

We begin with the brand-new title you've been eagerly awaiting from the incomparable Ann Major. *Love Me True,* our May MAN OF THE MONTH, is a riveting reunion romance offering the high drama and glamour that are Ann's hallmarks.

The enjoyment continues in FORTUNE'S CHILDREN: THE BRIDES with *The Groom's Revenge* by Susan Crosby. A young working woman is swept off her feet by a wealthy CEO who's married her with more than love on his mind—he wants revenge on the father who never claimed her, Stuart Fortune. A "must read" for all you fans of Daphne Du Maurier's *Rebecca!*

Barbara McMahon's moving story *The Cowboy and the Virgin* portrays the awakening—both sensual and emotional—of an innocent young woman who falls for a ranching Romeo. But can she turn the tables and corral *him?* Beverly Barton's emotional miniseries 3 BABIES FOR 3 BROTHERS concludes with *Having His Baby.* Experience the birth of a father as well as a child when a rugged rancher is transformed by the discovery of his secret baby—and the influence of his pretty mom. Then, in her exotic SONS OF THE DESERT title, *The Solitary Sheikh,* Alexandra Sellers depicts a hard-hearted sheikh who finds happiness with his daughters' aristocratic tutor. And *The Billionaire's Secret Baby* by Carol Devine is a compelling marriage-of-convenience story.

Now more than ever, Silhouette Desire offers you the most passionate, powerful and provocative of sensual romances. Make yourself merry this May with all six Desire novels—and buy another set for your mom or a close friend for Mother's Day!

Enjoy!

Joan Marlow Golan
Senior Editor, Silhouette Desire

Please address questions and book requests to:
Silhouette Reader Service
U.S.: 3010 Walden Ave., P.O. Box 1325, Buffalo, NY 14269
Canadian: P.O. Box 609, Fort Erie, Ont. L2A 5X3

ANN MAJOR
LOVE ME TRUE

SILHOUETTE *Desire*®

Published by Silhouette Books

America's Publisher of Contemporary Romance

To my late father, Millard Holland Major,
who taught me to love the written word

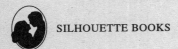 **SILHOUETTE BOOKS**

ISBN 0-373-76213-5

LOVE ME TRUE

Copyright © 1999 by Ann Major

This edition published by arrangement with Harlequin Books S.A.

® and TM are trademarks of Harlequin Books S.A., used under license. Trademarks indicated with ® are registered in the United States Patent and Trademark Office, the Canadian Trade Marks Office and in other countries.

Look us up on-line at: http://www.romance.net

Printed in U.S.A.

Books by Ann Major

ANN MAJOR

loves writing romance novels as much as she loves reading them. She is a proud mother of three children, who are now in high school and college. She lists hiking in the Colorado mountains with her husband, playing tennis, sailing, enjoying her cats and playing the piano among her favorite activities.

Dear Reader,

I love writing for the MAN OF THE MONTH promotional miniseries in Silhouette Desire, and I'm especially honored that my hero Joey Fasano is Desire's 125th MAN OF THE MONTH!

If I could have three wishes, one of them would be to hop into my man's brain, so I could figure out once and for all what makes him do and say all those illogical things that drive me crazy. Writing from the male point of view is the next best thing.

I think I get a little carried away with this sometimes. I tend to invent heroes who are larger-than-life, difficult and pushy. My guys love deeply and completely, especially when they don't want to. They have trouble with the "no" word. They want what they want, and they go after it. In short, they are every bit as maddeningly adorable as the real man in my life.

No fantasy haunts me more than the man from the past showing up on the heroine's doorstep and turning her life topsy-turvy.

My hero in this latest story, Joey Fasano, bad boy turned movie star, has become a force unto himself. He's never forgotten Heather, his first love, and once he sees her again, he realizes how empty his life and soul are without her. He can't go on, if he doesn't win her. Such a love is worth fighting for.

I hope you enjoy Joey and Heather's story.

Best,

Ann Major

Prologue

Maybe everybody was right after all. Maybe Joey Fasano was too wild and too passionate and too damned no-account for his own good.

Whatever.

Joey was too scared about Heather to care one way or the other.

The weather was as blustery and uncertain as his foul mood. It was raining intermittently. Every so often, the moon would break out from its wispy cover and put a stop to the nonsense.

Joey was damn sure driving like a demon from hell. His knuckles shone like bright white bones as he whipped the steering wheel to the right and swerved his daddy's battered Chevy onto the wet hospital drive.

Massive and ink-black, the rectangular building looked as forbidding as a prison as it loomed in stark relief above a black fringe of live-oak trees and was backlit by that violent, moon-dark, Texas sky.

Heather was in there somewhere…maybe dying.

His gut cramped in sick, demoralizing fear. Her powerful family would stop at nothing to keep him from seeing her.

Let them try.

He slammed on the brakes, got out of the car he'd taken without permission and ran, heedless of the soft rain that had begun to fall again, uncaring that he'd left the door wide open and the headlights blazing into the empty blackness like twin cones.

With a callused brown hand, he shielded his eyes against flashing red and white lights of an ambulance. More sirens screamed from the distant interstate, jarring him in his panicky confusion as raced toward the E.R. entrance.

His mouth twisted when he spotted the same scowling deputy who'd all but accused him of killing Ben a week ago. Ben, his best friend; Ben, Heather's brother. Ben, whose lifeless head he'd cradled in his lap. Ben, whose grave he'd visited less than an hour ago to plead for forgiveness.

Nod. Smile at the uniformed jerk. Stay cool.

Joey shot the officer a tense grin that must have passed muster. Then he shouldered his way through the sliding glass doors like a surly outlaw. Inside, heads swiveled as rain dripped off his black hair. He slicked the thick stuff back, out of his scalding eyes. A pretty teenager gasped coyly and then gave him one of those fluttery smiles all the girls gave him. He saw her father's hand clench warningly on her slim shoulder and draw her out of Joey's path.

Half boy, half man, Joey moved too fast, as if he hadn't quite grown accustomed to his long, rugged body. Still, he was hunky and gorgeous. His voracious sex appeal made him suspect with all parents and teachers, and with any other guy his age who had a girlfriend.

"You're every teenage girl's dream lover and every daddy's worst nightmare," Coach Howard had teased him when he'd been voted Most Handsome in high school.

"When I was your age I had pimples. I envy the hell out of you, kid. Looks like yours will open all sorts of doors."

Behind a cluttered desk a nurse ignored a stack of charts and blinking lights on her phone and licked pizza crust off her fingers.

But she couldn't ignore him.

No woman ever could, especially if he smiled.

But when he tried, the skin on either side of his mouth tightened painfully.

"Save the fake charm. Visiting hours are over, sonny."

She obviously had a teenage daughter.

Joey froze. "Please, Ma'am.... I've gotta find somebody.... She's real sick."

The nurse shook her head in curt dismissal, sucked a last crumb, and then punched a button on her telephone to tend to more important business.

Joey's cold wet hand grabbed the receiver from her.

"Heather Wade," he rasped, suddenly seeming older and scarier than his twenty years. "The senator's daughter.... What room is she in?"

"Your pretty face has got you way too cocky, sonny. You may be hot stuff to some little girls foolish enough to go for tall and dark and dangerous, but a Wade wouldn't wipe her pretty feet on the likes of you...even if you did get her pregnant."

His broad shoulders sagged. Joey's tough stance wilted. "Where—?" he pleaded in a desperate, breathless voice, a boy's voice now.

Her stare hardened. Then she seized the phone from him. "Get outta here, sonny, before you get yourself into real trouble. The senator's been down here. He told me all about you and to be on the watch-out—"

When Joey didn't budge, she hollered off-handedly, "Officer! It's him! It's that Joey Fasano guy."

Joey took off in a dead run.

So did the deputy.

As Joey sprinted like a crazed rat through a maze of endless white corridors, the big deputy lumbered at his heels.

The bastard would probably throw the book at him.

Let him. All that mattered was finding Heather...before it was too late.

Then Joey slammed through a double set of swinging doors only to find himself trapped in a dead-end hall on the seventh floor.

His heart beat like a tom-tom when he pivoted wildly just as the deputy banged through the doors and smiled.

Behind Joey, Senator Wade's voice thundered, ''What the hell are you doing up here, Fasano?''

''I came to see Heather.''

''Over my dead body, punk.''

Shock and disapproval rippled through the grim clump of fashionably-dressed people standing outside Heather's door.

''You better let me see her!'' Joey screamed *her* name like a crazy man. *''Heather!''*

Heather's mother opened the door. ''She doesn't want to see you.''

''You're lying!''

Vaguely Joey was aware of her mother's pitying gaze as he stumbled past her. Suddenly he felt that he moved in weird slow motion. The white walls closed in on him like a surrealistic nightmare.

Was that frail, thin creature veiled in curtains and swaddled in white sheets like a mummy in that far corner really his lively Heather?

The blinds were down. The room was gray and shadowy.

''Babe.... What have they done....'' He choked. His voice died. ''Oh, God...what have I done?''

Her amethyst eyes that usually brightened at the sight of him, were dull and painfilled. Dark circles of grief and exhaustion ringed them. She stared at him as if he were a ghost. Then she twisted her head away from him and lay as still as death.

Even in this state, he thought she was the prettiest girl in the world. He sat down beside her and took her slim hand. A shock went through him. Her fingers cold and stiff and lifeless. Just as Ben's had been.

"You okay, babe?"

"I'm fine," she whispered.

Fine? Her tone cut him. Ever after he would hate that word.

There was scarcely a pulsebeat in her slender, blue-veined wrist. Her icy skin was almost translucent.

She was so changed, so lifeless, fear squeezed his heart like a vice.

"Please...just go away," she whispered in a strange almost thready voice.

He lifted her hand and laced his brown fingers through hers. "What about our baby?"

Her voice broke on a sob. "There is no baby."

His own eyes filled with tears. Fighting them, he squeezed her hand and held on tightly. He gasped for air. He gasped again. He felt like a drowning man with nothing to hold on to. "But—"

"I want you out of my life, Joey. It's the only way."

"Heather." He felt sick at his stomach and unable to breathe in the dark, airless room. "You listen to me. We're still getting married—"

"No," she said in a rehearsed, robotlike tone. "I want to start over...fresh."

"With some rich guy like Roth that your daddy—"

"Daddy says if this gets out, me having been pregnant, people won't understand. They'll judge *him*. He says that I've been difficult my whole life."

"He's difficult and demanding. Not you. You're not supposed to be some perfect doll who follows all his orders. You'll shrivel up and die...if you do that."

"He says that just this once I need to think about him and act like a normal daughter, that I have to do the predictable, respectable things, that I have to finish school…and…and forget you."

"Yeah. Well, you tell him it's not that easy. 'Cause I won't ever, ever forget you. And I won't ever let you forget me, either."

"Don't make this harder, Joey. Please— If you and I hadn't dated, Ben would still be alive."

"Is that what *they* say? What *he* says?"

"I can't hurt them any more than I already have, especially Daddy, especially right now."

"It's not like I planned Ben's death or I wanted to get you pregnant," Joey cried. "I didn't want to hurt them. I love you."

He felt her fingertips flick through his thick, black hair that had probably dried into unruly tangles and then withdraw as if she were afraid to touch him because she wanted to so much. "Daddy says I've gotten into more trouble than ten kids."

"You haven't gotten into nearly as much trouble as me, babe," he said, attempting his old teasing tone.

"Daddy says you're a bad influence."

The soft finality in her stone-calm voice as she kept quoting her daddy killed something inside him.

"I thought you loved me."

Slowly she unlaced their joined fingers and shut her eyes.

"Heather—"

Tears leaked through her lashes and wet her white cheeks.

"Heather…."

She bit her lips.

"Don't do this, babe. Don't leave me. You know I can't make it without you. You're all I've got. All I ever want. You're everything."

The door opened. "Fasano, you've had your time with

her. Now get the hell out of here before I sic the law on you.''

Her father was standing beside Laurence Roth in the doorway. Her other relatives were peering at him like he was some kind of wild beast they'd run to ground and were about to slaughter.

''You all think you know so much. You don't know her. You're killing her. You're killing both of us.''

''Get out, Fasano, before I lose my patience. You've already cost me one child. You'd better leave quick, boy, before I decide to use my considerable power to break you for what you've done to Heather.''

''Joey....'' *Her* pleading whisper came from behind him. Joey turned back to Heather. Her eyes were closed, and tears streamed silently down her cheeks. ''Go....''

He'd hurt her. He'd made her cry. Her family had never thought he was good enough. She'd always hated having to sneak around to see him. Now, because of Ben and the baby, they really hated him.

He'd lost her. How would he go on? He wasn't rich or important like they were. She was everything to him. Everything.

More than anything, he wanted to take her into his arms and hold her till she stopped crying. He wanted to press his head into her breasts, to rock her back and forth, to never let her go. Travis Wade would probably kill him if he touched her.

Joey tossed his head back at a cocky angle and swaggered past Wade and Roth with the silent, insolent pride of a kid who had nothing else.

Joey didn't know where he was going.

Without Heather, he didn't care.

All he knew was that he was leaving Texas. And he wasn't coming back till he was as rich and powerful as all of these arrogant bastards.

Then he'd make them pay.

One

A lot of smart people don't believe in the devil, but Heather Wade knew better. Because sure as shooting, the very same devil who sent the snake to Eve also sent Joey Fasano slithering her way. It was easy for other rich girls whose daddies were senators to be good. It was hard for Heather.

Impossible when Joey was around. He brought out the worst in her. That's why she'd fallen in love with him as a girl.

That's why she was determined to forget him now that she was a full-grown woman on the verge of matrimony.

Tall and broad-shouldered, black-eyed and black-haired, Joey Fasano had been born sinfully handsome. He'd been as smolderingly intense as a box-office sensation years before he became one.

Maybe some seven-year-old little girls would not have found the various sorts of devilment he proposed in his hideout as exciting as she. Not all would have thought it a lark to snatch the Reverend Scott's wife's lacy panties off her clothesline after Joey pointed out how they snapped like a fat pirate's pantaloons in the wind. But then it never did take much more than a sexy wink and devil-may-care grin to show her how much more fun the crooked path with the likes of him was than the straight and narrow with more staid folk.

And now, six years after she'd given that gorgeous snake in hunk's clothing up for good, whose scalding eyes should be burning a hole out of her television screen and setting her blood afire?

Ignore those coal-bright dark eyes fringed with dense sable lashes.

Ignore how they made her feel singed to the core and shivery and alive for the first time in years.

Somehow the way Joey looked at her was more real than anything in her bedroom, more substantial than the Aubusson carpet she was curled up on, more sensual than the glass of red wine and the tall, black bottle beside the untidy pile of bridal magazines stacked on her low table, more tantalizing than the red chiffon skirt that fell so softly over her long, shapely legs.

She stared at that shock of black hair tumbling across his dark brow, her wayward heart thumping as eagerly as a hungry rabbit's who'd seen a carrot. Every time Joey whispered her name, she punched the pause button and gasped for breath.

Turn him off. Go to bed.

No way.

This wasn't the first time her life had swerved disastrously off course because of Joey. Not that she was about to admit, even to herself, that it had.

One minute she had been a normal bride-to-be returning home from one of those stuffy society affairs. Bored and tired, she'd stepped into her vast bedroom with the familiar, rose wallpaper, high ceilings, antebellum furniture, and tall windows. Then she'd punched a button on her answering machine and her mother's shrill voice had jolted her into this new reality. Until then Heather had convinced herself she really could marry Larry Roth and make Daddy, who was up for re-election, very happy.

That was before Joey Fasano, bad-boy movie star, had stomped back into her life with his usual vengeance.

Except for Joey, nobody had ever known, least of all her parents, what to make of their mercurial, free-spirited, unpredictable daughter. As a baby she'd gotten into so much mischief during naptime—like the afternoon she'd pushed a stool to the stove, stood on her tiptoes, and turned on the gas jets because they smelled funny—that her mother had been forced to tie a net over her crib.

Not that a net and a few red satin tie-downs could contain a spirit as lively as the nimble-fingered Heather's. The very next afternoon she escaped her netted prison and poured all the soap powder onto the bathroom floor and played in it like it was a sand pile.

If the adult Heather had a bad case of bridal jitters after her mother's message, maybe it was natural under the circumstances.

It isn't every night that your old boyfriend, who just happens to be the sexiest movie star in the universe, wins an Oscar and throws your life into a tailspin. Leave it to Joey to clasp that golden statuette to his heart and confess to millions in that low, choked voice that he couldn't forget her.

Not that she'd caught his memorable performance live. No, to please her mother she'd hosted a fund-raiser and had taped the show. She'd come home exhausted only to be drawn into Joey's seductive web by that little red message light.

Her mother had been frantic.

How come Joey Fasano, the big, bad movie star, thanked you, you of all people? My daughter? How come he said you were unforgettable? You promised you wouldn't see him again! Have you been in contact with him, Heather Ann? Your father's very upset. Call me. We have to talk. Oh, this is your mother. I don't care how late you get in. Call!

Heather hadn't won her unpredictable, mercurial stripes by doing what her mother told her. She yanked the phone off the hook, kicked off her high heels, and fast-forwarded the videotape. Sinking to the floor, she watched Joey collect his prize—over and over again, scarcely daring to breathe. Every time, he rasped her name and then the word, *unforgettable.* In fact, even though she was headachy with exhaustion, she might have watched him again if a twig hadn't scratched her barred window.

Her hand froze on the remote, her nerves responding on some instinctive, primitive level. With a keenly honed ear for danger she strained forward, listening to the night sounds outside the mansion. There was only the wind rushing through the trees along the bayou. Only the distant hoot of a solitary owl. Then a tugboat's light flashed through the avenue of oaks, and lurid shadows leapt against her window shade.

She jumped up, thinking to race to the hall to check on Nicky again.

The dark shape dissolved. Nothing was out there. They weren't in any real danger as they had been two years ago. She reminded herself of the high fences girdling the grounds, of the bodyguard patrolling those fences.

Unforgettable, rasped Joey's low voice in her tired, incredulous brain.

Joey was the reason she was so jumpy. It had taken her years to get over him. Not that it was easy; he was America's number one sex symbol. Posters of him in skin-tight black leather were plastered all over the world.

Joey doesn't matter. Who cares what he said about you tonight on national television.

You are in Louisiana a million miles away from him, a million worlds away from him. You are getting married. He's a movie star. You're a single mom. He forgot you years ago.

Heather wasn't used to wine, or the almost mystical clarity it can bring to confused thoughts and repressed emotions. Her cheeks were flushed. Her long-lashed violet eyes were misty as she felt things and knew things she'd refused to deal with—like the real reason for the string of unsuitable boyfriends that had followed Joey till she'd finally settled on Larry.

Her father was worried about the upcoming election. She lifted a snapshot of Nicky and shivered at the thought of what Joey might do if he found out she had a son.

Not *if.*

When.

Men like Joey Fasano should come with warning labels tattooed on their foreheads at birth—*too sexy to handle.* Or *danger—testosterone overload.* Girls with too many hormones should be locked up in a nunnery till they were wise enough to deal with boys like Joey.

From the second he'd crawled out of his cradle and cast his moody-broody, black eyes on Heather, who'd lived on the ranch next to his, he had oozed way too much charm for a girl of her madcap, irreverent nature to resist.

Six years ago, Heather had finally come to her senses and had told him to get out of her life or else—*or else* being her father. Until tonight, when Joey had seared her with his megawatt, know-it-all grin and thanked her—*her*—on live television, she would have sworn they were through with each other forever.

After all, she was marrying the man of her father's dreams in a week.

After all, Joey had made tabloid headlines recently by fishing the world's most gorgeous supermodel naked out of his swimming pool.

But Joey had cradled his Oscar to his chest like a baby as he'd hunched over the podium and thanked first the Academy, his agent, and his director. Joey had gone blank for a second. Then he'd thanked *her,* Heather, the girl from his past, instead of the Lady Godiva of the tabloids.

He'd said *she* was *unforgettable.*

Dear God. Heather didn't want anything Joey Fasano said or did to affect her ever again. His charm was superficial; his taste in women trashy.

Heather was an heiress, a retired photojournalist, a philanthropist, a mother. Her fairy-tale life was perfect *without* him.

Right.

Her life was a charade. She was such a consummate actress, she sometimes fooled even herself.

Static flickered on the silent screen of Heather's television.

Why had she taped the Academy Awards show tonight, of all nights, when she had known Joey was up for Best Actor?

Why hadn't she ignored her messages and gone to bed? Why wouldn't his raspy voice stop inside her brain?

Why? Why? Why? Nothing about her feelings for Joey had ever made sense. Except they were intense. So intense, she'd been running from them for years.

Thus, Heather sat huddled in a ball of misery beside the low table in her bedroom chewing the red nail polish off her long fingernails as she obsessed about Joey. Without thinking she slid two photographs together on the polished oak surface so that the smiling dark faces of the identical little boys lay side by side.

At the startling resemblance, she whitened. Huge dark eyes. Devil-may-care grins. Matching cowlicks over their left temples.

Now that she was moving back to Texas, sooner or later, Joey was bound to find out. She understood her fear. But she didn't want to think about why Joey had stirred her so deeply on other levels.

Heather Ann, promise us you won't ever tell Joey about Nicky.

Her parents and Julia had looked so white and stricken as they'd stood beside Nicky's crib that she'd promised…again.

Heather's long, golden, wavy hair was swept away from her solemn face into an elegant chignon. Her mother's diamonds glittered at her throat. With her bare feet tucked beneath the red gown and her lips free of lipstick, she looked more like the disheveled wild-child Joey had loved than the sophisticated young woman of society at the fund-raiser.

Images, especially those on film, always affected her too profoundly. The particular pictures that quickened her pulse were of five-year-old little boys with curly black hair and jet-dark eyes that flashed with mischief as they dangled upside down from a tree.

A stranger would have thought the pictures were of the same boy. But Heather had taken one twenty years ago beside the clear waters of a spring-fed creek in central Texas and the other only yesterday on the muddy bank of the brown bayou in her backyard.

A stillness descended upon her as she touched the yellowed photograph of the boy in ragged cutoffs.

''Joey—''

He'd been an innocent boy then. Tonight, the man had seemed painfully bitter and edgily dangerous.

When she brought his picture to her lips, a single tear traced down her cheek.

Once the only man for her had been Joey Fasano. Joey, who kissed with his eyes closed. Joey, who was a bad boy by day but whose face was as innocent as an angel's when he slept.

Joey's teasing black eyes that had always looked straight into hers and recognized her true self.

The soft, damp Louisiana air was warm and scented with roses and rain as it sifted across the wide verandas of Belle Christine, once her grandmother's home, now hers. Perhaps it was the antebellum mansion standing proudly on its slight rise behind the Mississippi's levee, surrounded by ancient live oaks dripping with moss, that made Heather feel not only her fear but the past and Joey's appeal so keenly. For old houses have a timelessness, a link to the past, that modern homes lack. Suddenly the poor, ambitious boy with his head full of dreams seemed far more real to her than the polished mahogany surface of the antique escritoire beside her canopy bed or the bladelike leaves of the banana trees rustling outside against the exterior walls of her home.

Joey.

Again she was seventeen and the torn leather upholstery on the backseat of Joey's ancient Chevy was scratching her bare thighs. Joey's hands fumbled with the buttons of her blouse while his hot mouth explored the sweet mysteries of her body. For as long as she could remember, the highborn Heather Wade had felt the lowborn Joey Fasano pulsing in her blood.

Forget him.

Your love for him nearly destroyed you and everybody you loved.

At twenty-six, Heather was beautiful, rich, and envied by all. She was high society. Big rich. Texas royalty. Her father, who put money and power above all else, had set up a trust fund for her so she would never have to worry about money again. Her stolid bridegroom was ambitious.

But there was a shadow-side to her seemingly perfect life. A childhood illness had taken her older sister, Alison, when she was ten; later, her brother, Ben, had died in a car wreck. As her parents' sole surviving child, Heather felt enormous pressure to make them happy.

In her third year as a photojournalist, Heather had taken a picture that had won her a Pulitzer. But the coveted prize that should have made her career, had ended it. When she'd announced her retirement, jealous colleagues had been exultant. Her family had been equally thrilled. Only Joey had called to ask what was wrong. Shaking, she'd slammed the phone down. When it had rung again, she'd run outside to avoid hearing it.

She twisted her diamond engagement ring till it cut her finger. She had to put Joey out of her mind.

Most girls would have given anything to be marrying Laurence. Her mother kept telling her that marriage would complete her as her career hadn't. Thus, when Laurence, who was older and wiser, had led her into the purple shade of the camphor tree in her rose garden, she had not resisted when his arrogant gaze had held hers while his cold hands slipped an engagement ring on her finger.

Laurence had bought a house high in the hills overlooking Austin and signed the deed over to her as a wedding gift. He had given her carte blanche with the finest decorator in Texas. Her thrilled mother had since taken charge.

Numbly Heather had addressed a thousand engraved wedding invitations. Ten bridesmaids' dresses had been created out of exquisite pink brocade. They would honeymoon in Maui. Julia had obtained a sabbatical from her order to care for Nicky during the wedding festivities and honeymoon.

Everybody told Heather she was the luckiest girl alive. She sucked in a quick breath, picked up the VCR remote control, and defiantly jabbed Rewind, pausing on Joey's face. For a long moment, she stared at the television, her glazed, intense emotions blinding her so that she saw nothing and heard nothing. Somehow in that crushing silence as Joey's features wobbled, invisible defenses inside her began to crumble.

She had fallen in love with Joey years before their adventures in his Chevy. When she was five he'd invited her to his hideout and seduced her into that game of doctor that had resulted in endless lectures from her mother and father, who had told her Joey was worse than his drunken father.

But Joey had been too much fun to resist. Despite their fathers, Heather's clandestine friendship with Joey had blossomed into love.

Then Ben had died, and so had her world.

Later, after Joey had become a world-famous movie star, she'd figured he'd forgotten her. Even when Joey had returned to Wimberley, the town they'd grown up in, and started buying land despite her own powerful father's attempt to stop him, she'd clung to that illusion. Hadn't he snubbed her the two times she'd seen him on the town square?

Then tonight, in front of millions, Joey had gone and done this wild and crazy thing that touched her wild and crazy heart.

Heather's frantic gaze swept to her white, virginal wedding dress and its faux Renaissance beaded bridal cap and veil which hung in a plastic bag on a high hook above half a dozen hand-tooled leather suitcases. Next she looked at her camera equipment, stacked in a separate pile of black duffel bags in a distant corner since she was unsure about taking them.

All was in readiness for the long drive to the Texas hill country tomorrow.

Heather tipped the wine bottle and refilled her goblet for the fourth time. She barely felt the thin, cool crystal against her lips; barely tasted the warm red wine that slid too easily down her throat.

Tears pooled in her violet eyes as she touched the play button.

Dear God, why am I doing this to myself?

It's 2:00 a.m. I've got a long drive tomorrow. And I'm not a morning person.

Heather's head throbbed. She felt tense and achy. Four photograph albums from her high school days, loose pictures, mostly of Joey, spilling out of them, lay in a tumble at her feet. Looking through them had brought back the past, had made her weepily nostalgic. Joey had loved her. Truly loved her.

Go to bed.

She shook her bright head and gripped the remote control.

Play it again, Sam....

Heather was still trembling when Joey Fasano's molten image blazed into focus.

Lord. He was magic on film. She was the first to be bowled over by him, to capture his special magic with a camera. If ever a rugged, male face was created to arouse and seductively provoke the female mating instinct, Joey's was.

He's trash. Like his father.

But as irresistible as dark, gooey chocolate.

Dusky skin stretched over ruthless, rawboned features. And, oh, why had God given him that sensual, kissable mouth that could tempt a girl to madness? Even on television Joey's intense, black eyes burned too deeply and too hotly. His devastatingly bitter smile saw through her rich girl defenses and made her pulse skitter.

Get a life.

He'll hurt you again; hurt your family; hurt Nicky even more.

You belong to Laurence.

Heather stared wordlessly at Joey whose long hair was tied at the nape in a ponytail. The tuxedo accentuated the breadth of his powerful shoulders and the narrowness of his waist. She was keenly aware of dangerous, sinewy muscles rippling beneath well-cut cloth.

The rough boy she'd loved was gone. This new, older, elegant version was somehow leaner, meaner, smoother, tougher. A darkness had entered this man's soul and etched into the hard planes of his arrogant face. He had played pirates, bikers, gypsies, warriors, mercenaries—irreverent, unrepentant scoundrels all of them. This battleworn giant who lit big screens with his smoldering love scenes and know-it-all smiles was a stranger.

So, why after all these years could the mere sight of this embittered warrior and his saying she was unforgettable make her head pound and her womb ache? Her throat go dry? Her brain go comatose?

His raspy voice mocked her.

No more wine for you, babe.

If only he didn't look so much like her darling Nicky.

Their uncanny resemblance turned her skin to gooseflesh.

Beneath dark, slashing brows, Joey's hot black eyes seared and seduced her. His gaze lured her with promises even as he kept his own dangerous secrets.

Heather's palms grew clammy.

No more dangerous than her own secrets.

His companion of the night, supermodel Daniella Wolfe, was slim and tall. With masses of gold ringlets and huge violet eyes, Daniella meant to dazzle.

She looks like me. Why do his girlfriends always look like me?

Again Joey's roughened voice scoffed. *Don't flatter yourself, babe. What's it to you if I dig leggy blondes?*

Heather's head buzzed when Joey leaned too far back in his seat just like he'd done in high school to taunt the teachers when he hadn't known the answers. His gorgeous mouth was curled into that same cocky smile he'd worn when her rich crowd had snubbed him because of his bad clothes.

Even if you won't tell your father about us, you aren't ever going to forget me, Heather Wade...or what we did together...in bed...in the woods...in my hideout.

Her hands fisted against her chiffon-clad thigh. *Yes, I will. I will, too, forget you, Joey. I have forgotten—*

God created me just for you, babe.

"Maybe the devil put a hex on me," she'd replied sassily.

The reverend once called me the devil's spawn. You're mine.

Joey had been the first boy to kiss Heather full on the mouth. The first boy to French kiss her. Indeed, he had claimed plenty of those long, wet kisses before seducing Heather when she'd been a naive seventeen. At eighteen, he'd been a virgin, too. There had been lots of firsts with Joey.

Lots of firsts. Lots of only's.

From what she'd read in the tabloids, Joey no longer discriminated when it came to women. He had a revolving bedroom door. He was Hollywood's sexiest, reigning superstud.

So—that's his business!

The next camera shot zoomed in on the number one sex goddess who stood up on the stage holding an envelope. Strobe lights flashed behind her. The world-famous actress with the little girl voice looked like she'd poured her voluptuous body into a sequined, tubelike black gown that was slit to her navel. Beside her towered the biggest cowboy star in the business.

The long slim envelope was ripped open.

"—the nominees for Best Actor are—"

Heather gripped the remote control harder as the names of films and stars were read in the actress's feather-soft tone.

"—the winner is—"

Applause exploded in the auditorium, drowning out the end of her sentence.

Joey's name pulsed through Heather as she lifted her

empty wineglass and then set it down, resisting the temptation to refill it again.

Now. *Now he would go white with shock and then swagger up to the stage, stare into the camera with his bleak, level gaze and say it.*

Heather's breath stalled in her lungs.

No more. Turn it off. Don't put yourself through it again.

The camera followed the tall, dark man striding down the aisle with pantherlike grace in his elegant tux. The audience rose and gave him a thundering ovation.

Heather's blood heated in anticipation.

You got it bad, babe.

Still, her violet eyes remained glued to his powerful image.

The moment she had been waiting for came all too soon.

After thanking the Academy, his agent, and his director, Joey grew quiet. For a long, intense moment, he continued to stand before his spellbound audience. He shifted his weight from one foot to the other. As his silence lengthened, he looked odd and blank-faced and suddenly very ill at ease. His dark face paled. Hard lines bracketed his mouth. His grip tightened threateningly on his gold-plated statuette.

For a tough guy, he sure looked afraid.

Every bit as afraid as he'd looked that night in the hospital.

Still, without speaking, he leaned into the mike. Glaring white light bathed his chiseled features. A muscle in his tanned cheek twitched as if long-suppressed emotions raged so close to the surface he couldn't hold them back.

Then his cynical black gaze targeted her, and his deep, raspy voice wrapped her. For an instant he was that unsure, cocky boy she'd loved, and they were the only two people in the world.

Terror gripped her. Once that special, measured look had been meant for her alone. The only time she'd ever seen his hard features go still like that was right before he shut his eyes to kiss her. As he stared at the cameras, he broke into that special smile that had belonged only to her.

The smile died.

"I wish I had someone in my personal life to thank. But I don't. God, here I am. You'd think I was the luckiest guy alive. But hell… I'm probably the loneliest."

He had been a lonely little boy, too.

Joey had been bean-pole skinny in ragged, dirty jeans that always rode too high on his ankles. His hair had hung long and lank. Scorned by the teachers, ridiculed by the other kids. She remembered the way he'd sat hunched over in the back of the classroom, reading books he'd checked out of the school library to escape the bitter reality of his childhood. She remembered how sometimes she'd used her ballpoint pen to shoot spitwads at him. How once she'd hit Mrs. Vanderfort who'd then pounced on Joey. How he'd taken the abuse with an insolent smile and then later teased her. "Someday, Heather, I'll make you pay for your crimes."

The man on television stood up straighter. His deep tone roughened. His fathomless black eyes bored into her. "But there is someone…someone who has proved to be… unforgettable. So, Heather…. Babe, if you're out there, I'm gonna thank you right now because I may never get another chance to. You were the first person to ever believe in me. The only real— I wish…we could go back and start—" He sounded choked. "Oh, God—"

Flushing darkly, he turned to the half-naked goddess in the slit gown. "I'm making one helluva fool of myself over a woman who threw—" Then, as if he suddenly realized the magnitude of what he'd so publicly revealed, he ducked his black head and bolted off the stage. The crowd stood up and cheered him as he ran for cover. The only person not standing and not clapping was the breathtaking Daniella. When he sat down beside her and reached for her hand, she snatched it away to finger the diamonds at her throat.

Heather's eyes were burning as she punched the remote, freezing Joey's stark visage on her screen.

Indomitable pride was carved into his strong, handsome face. Stubborn rebellion. But there was anguish, too. His genuine pain wrapped around her heart and wouldn't let go. She felt a shuddering deep within herself.

Both her parents and the town they had grown up in had despised him for being Deo Fasano's son. Joey had felt less than nothing in that town. Maybe now he had the world's acclaim, but tonight she had seen an even deeper pain in his eyes than she'd seen when she'd told him goodbye in the hospital.

Don't do this, babe. Don't leave me. You know I can't make it without you.

Her grief and guilt over Ben had been so profound, she'd blocked out his pain.

Thank God, he'd made it…without her.

Heather wanted to call him and congratulate him—

No.

He'd called her, hadn't he, when she'd won the—

When he'd asked her what was wrong, she'd hung up on him. He'd called back. She hadn't picked up, but when he'd rasped his number into her recorder, she'd written it down.

There had been nights when she'd pulled it out and looked at it as if it were some last link to him.

Quit staring at that oversexed, conceited, rebellious, hot-blooded man who couldn't keep his hands out of your pants. Don't even think about calling him.

You can't stop thinking about me, babe. If you marry anybody but me… I'll haunt you in your bed. There'll be three of us on your wedding night.…

Funny, how every time she kissed Larry, that obnoxious raspy voice of Joey's started heckling her.

He doesn't quite have my knack, now does he, babe?

But that would stop.

She was going to do what was expected of her for once and be happy about it. The well-ordered structure of Laurence's life would smooth any rough edges in her being. Nicky, who had been asking why he didn't have a father, would have one. Julia could relax and give her entire soul to her chosen vocation. Heather's parents would be thrilled to have her respectably married.

A shadow passed over her face as she thought of how much her mother and father had suffered. It was up to Heather to make it up to them.

But her tears wouldn't quit as she stared at the torture in Joey's frozen face.

Joey had been able to read her heart and her forbidden fantasies with unerring accuracy. Once his wild, quirky soul had been a perfect match for hers. He had been her best friend. He had shared every thought that was in his heart as Laurence, who worked long hours at his law practice, never did.

That was then.

This was now.

Her love for Joey had come at a terrible price.

Joey was image; Laurence was substance. Hadn't her career taught her the terrible danger of confusing the two?

Joey's bedroom exploits in Hollywood were legendary.

Laurence was decent and reliable. He respected her. A happy marriage took time, work, commitment, and compromise. Sex appeal was the least important ingredient. She wanted to be safe. Larry was safe.

What about love? rasped that forbidden voice.

What about Nicky?

What would happen when Joey found out about Nicky?

Two

Joey. Daniella. Mac.

Superstar. Supermodel. Superagent.

The fallout from what Joey had said and done on stage surrounded the three passengers in the stretch limo like a poisonous gas as they sped through the night dark. Mac's handsome black face smoldered with enigmatic misery as he stared out the window at the whizzing headlights.

If Joey was red-faced and guilty with self-loathing, Daniella's dark silence was equally oppressive as the sleek, black car pulled up in front of L.A.'s trendiest restaurant where Mac was throwing Joey a party.

Her dark brows knitting, Daniella turned on Joey. Then the screaming crowd rushed the car, their hoarse cries drowning out her outburst.

Thank God. Joey was in no mood for another tongue-lashing.

Joey had slouched against the door while Mac had tried to cajole Danny out of her mood by praising her latest

Vogue cover, but she'd stiffened and notched her exquisite nose even higher.

Finally, even Mac lost patience. "Honey, give him a break. He's gonna have a hard enough time living that sappy speech down."

Daniella's glossily painted mouth had tightened. "His fans'll love it! Poor, poor Joey, pining for some long-lost love— How does that make *me* look?"

Joey had had it with Daniella. She hadn't even waited for the ceremony to end before she'd attacked.

As if he didn't despise himself enough. He didn't know why he'd thanked Heather. She was the last person he should have mentioned. She was marrying Larry Roth. He didn't give a damn about her anymore.

This was supposed to be the happiest night of *his* life. Instead, he'd stood on that stage, drinking in the applause, feeling the heat of the lights only to wonder why he felt no rush of exhilaration. He'd come so far, in such a short time. No way would he ever forget growing up as the town drunk's son, or his jobs as dishwasher, waiter, and bouncer. Or the cockroach-infested apartments in dangerous neighborhoods, or that awful opening night when he'd sunk so low he'd stripped naked in that back-alley play and then lost his nerve and leapt offstage. A producer had chased him with a video camera and caught a full frontal view. Joey had grabbed a lady's sweater and jammed it against his crotch while she shrieked. From time to time that clip was still played.

But Mac had been in the audience that night and had thought Joey was magic. Mac had tracked him down, gone to his apartment and rammed a fist on the front door.

"Who the hell are you?" Joey had demanded, putting the chain on at the sight of the huge, muscular black man looming in his doorway.

"Your agent."

"I'm through acting."

"Can we discuss that?" Mac's bright grin had been infectious. "You impressed me in *Hanging Out.*"

"You're impressing the hell out of my downstairs neighbor—"

Mac's dark face paled when he saw the plump little girl in black pigtails squatting on the top step, her big black eyes popping out on stems.

Mac glowered. "Quit eyeballing me, girl. Go beat a drum or play with a doll—"

"Selena," her mother yelled. "Get in here now."

Defiantly Selena marched down the stairs. When Mac stuck out his tongue and waggled fingers over his ears, she ran to her mother. "Mama! There's a man out here scaring me!"

"You gonna let me in before that woman calls the cops and they haul me to jail?"

Gut instinct made Joey lift the chain.

"How'd you know Selena's a drummer?"

"I've got three rug rats of my own."

"You're married?"

"To my high school sweetheart."

"True love…in this city?"

"Titania keeps me sane in this insane business."

Joey cracked the door wider. "I won't ever take my clothes off for a part again."

"How about a beer?"

They'd talked for hours. Mac had sworn he could make a big difference in Joey's career, and he had. Mac had seen that he met the right people, had taught him to quit overacting.

"Read the part a time or two, no more," Mac had commanded in his bullying, enthusiastic way. "Then just get out there and wing it. What you've got to do is play along with the other actors. Live it when you do it. Don't think so much. You're a natural."

Because of Mac and Titania, who were overzealous

about handling every aspect of Joey's life—his moods, his women and his money—Joey was at the top.

But other than Mac and Titania and their kids, Joey had no real friends. Suddenly on that stage tonight he'd felt as alone and empty as he had at the bottom, maybe lonelier.

Mac and Titania had each other. Sometimes their happiness made him even more aware of what was missing. Maybe that was why he'd started buying land in Texas.

"You could have thanked *me* up there—" Daniella had said to Joey in the limo.

God. Everything, everything was always about her.

"So— Thanks." Joey bit out the word.

"You treat me like I'm nothing to you, Joey."

"He sleeps with you, doesn't he?" Mac inserted.

Joey flinched and hoped Mac wouldn't catch the subtext in Danny's sudden silence and sly look.

What the hell was wrong with him? He was supposed to be a Hollywood superstud. Danny was one of the most beautiful women in the world. And he had no interest in sex. Before her, he'd dated girls a night or two, always dropping them when they demanded to be more than a decoration on his arm.

He could have anybody. Women were always handing him room keys, phone numbers, business cards. So—how come he didn't want them?

"You don't care about me though," Daniella persisted.

What did she expect? What was he to her but a celebrity stud she'd used to put herself on the map?

He hadn't asked Daniella to jump into his pool naked and scream she couldn't swim. She'd probably hired that paparazzi piece of trash to climb his tree and take that shot of her without a stitch on just as Joey had dragged her out of the water.

The next morning their "affair" and the incriminating photograph of him giving Daniella mouth to mouth resuscitation had made every tabloid cover in the civilized world.

Then she'd come on to him at a party with the line, "Everybody already thinks we're doing it, so why don't we?" Before he could cut her for being so pushy, she'd kissed him.

Second photo of their mouths and bodies glued together. More tabloids.

No use denying his involvement with her after that. The media had given the world a gripping image. Truth didn't matter. Would his fans believe photos they could salivate over with their own eyes—or what he told them?

A week later Daniella had bribed his gullible maid out of his beach house key. She'd climbed into his bed naked and kissed him. That night he'd almost lived up to his reputation as Hollywood's number one sex symbol.

So, she'd used him. Big damn deal. His fame made him fair game.

"You're a star. I'm a star. How come you say you're nothing," he murmured in her ear.

"I want more, Joey."

For no reason at all he thought of the drowsy summer afternoon he'd taught a golden-haired Heather to skim rocks across the creek. His stones had skipped to the other side; hers had gone *plunk*. But, oh, how they'd laughed— together. And, oh, what they'd done later in bed.

She was getting married in a week.

Maybe he wanted more, too.

"I've heard that before," he said to Daniella.

"I mean more…like a diamond ring."

"Marriage?"

Her silent face was as easy to read as a red neon light blinking *YES!*

"No way, baby."

Daniella's eyes went white-bright as she glared. "Go to hell, Joey."

"Been there. Done that. For six damn years."

He didn't know why the hell he'd said what he'd said on that stage. He'd just been standing up there with those hot kleig lights, sweating like a pig. His knees had buckled. He'd been so damned scared, he'd felt so damned alone. He'd blurted out the first stupid thing that hit him.

Heather— Again he saw Ben's bright, broken red car, saw her bend over Ben. When he'd tried to comfort her, she'd pushed him away, crying it was his fault. Then she'd let that cold, blue-blooded bastard, Larry Roth, fold her into his arms and lead her away.

Damn her hide for carving his heart out, for driving him to these crazy, airless heights to prove he wasn't just a worthless nobody.

After a pause he said to Daniella, "When I want to get married, I'll ask."

The fans' screams outside the limo roared louder. A young brunette hurled herself at his door and beat the glass with her fists.

"Let me in. I love you, Joey."

Join the world!

The fan mashed her breasts against the glass and squirmed.

Mac grinned. "Titania would skin me alive if she saw this—"

Mac was popular with the ladies. Not that he ever did more than look. Titania was notoriously jealous.

Joey became aware of the shrill cacophony of the crowd yelling for him to get out. Fans of all sizes and ages screamed.

"Stardom," Mac purred. "Your big dream's come true."

Joey laughed shortly.

"Be careful what you wish for?" Mac murmured. "What my other clients wouldn't give—"

This craziness was the price Joey paid, for doing the

work he loved, or would have loved, if they'd give him
roles with more depth. He was tired of his warrior roles
even though all his movies had been smash hits. He was
tired of every woman thinking he was a god in bed.

Louie, his bodyguard, opened the door and told them to
run. A blonde hurled herself at Mac. Gently, Mac deflected
her and flashed his wedding ring toward the cameras.

Joey dragged Daniella out of the car through the throng
behind him, shielding her from the worst with his muscular
body.

Flashbulbs popped, blinding him.

"Faster," he hissed over his shoulder when she stopped
and began to pull her dress down and stick her chest out,
simpering and flirting with the cameras.

"Smile for the nice man, Joey," Daniella ordered.

"Hug her!" a girl screamed.

"Kiss her!"

Encouraged, Daniella's hand snaked around his neck, her
red, gooey mouth covering his. "Kiss me, you undersexed
bastard. Make it look good. After all, you're an actor."

He fought her. For a second more her lips and arms
imprisoned him before he broke free.

Inside it was no better.

Mac's party was frantic. When Joey stepped through the
door, the music stopped. Everybody froze and stared. This
awkward interval was followed by a spontaneous burst of
applause started by a radiant Titania. In a room filled with
gazelle-thin beauties, Titania's buxom figure in her white-
sequined gown made her seem larger than life.

Joey nodded to her and then waved the guests to go back
to whatever they'd been doing. For a moment longer he
lingered at the entrance, watching Mac's endless number
of guests, mostly starlets—coming and going. They
crowded around Mac and Titania, standing three and four
deep at the bar. Mac and Titania were soon having the time
of their lives. Then the band started playing, and rock music

hit Joey like a tidal wave. Above that roar, people started yelling.

"Speech! Speech!"

"Thank me, Joey," a pretty girl teased.

Everybody laughed except Joey, whose grim smile got harder.

"Lonely, lonely superstud."

God— Suddenly a fierce yearning for bleached limestone hills and the creek with its woodsy smells made him ache for the peace and sanity of his Texas ranch.

"I'll go home with you, Joey," another girl whispered.

Joey's gut coiled tighter; his mouth twisted. Would he ever learn to handle this inconvenient side of fame—the constant stares, the never-ending invasion of his privacy? He walked straight into the room, engaging no one's eyes, especially no female's.

"Could I get you something, darling?" The girl who pounced had glossy black hair. Her laser-bright eyes made too many promises.

"I'm with someone."

"Not any more, lover." She pointed at the dance floor.

Joey spun. Daniella was dancing cheek to cheek, body to body with Zachary Ranch, his director.

Joey charged toward them. He hated like hell to be rude to Mac and Titania, but the strange, sick-at-heart mood that had gripped him on that stage had him wild with panic again. The only way he could stay here was to get wasted or stoned. He didn't do drugs, so he had to get out of this town. Out of this state. Back to Texas where people cut him down to human size. *Back to Texas before Heather got married.*

Joey pulled out his cell phone and punched in his pilot's number. His orders were brief.

Joey pocketed his flip-phone. "Let's go, Danny."

She snuggled against Zach.

Joey tapped her arm.

When Zach tried to ease her free, she clung like a magnet. "Zach and me, we're having fun."

"Stay then." Joey's dark tone implied he didn't care what she did. He was a little surprised when she followed him.

Outside, they had to run the gauntlet of his fans again. Much to Louie's dismay, when the mother of a little girl on crutches thrust a notebook toward Joey, he patiently signed it. Even though the crowd mobbed him, and Louie screamed for him to get in the car, Joey gave the little girl an encouraging word and a hug.

It took them thirty minutes to reach the airport. Howard, his pilot, was climbing aboard the Learjet and settling himself into the cockpit when the limo zoomed up.

Joey joined Howard and guided the jet down the runway until he got clearance to take off into a black, starlit sky. Reluctantly, he handed Howard the controls and went back to Daniella, who snapped her eyes shut and ignored him. He tossed his Oscar into a seat and sprawled at the other end of the jet. He slept all the way to Texas.

With only a few hours left of the night, they walked through the door of his ranch house.

He was opening windows to let in the smell of cedar and the warm, night air, when the phone rang.

Daniella grabbed it and then slammed it down.

"Who—?"

"Some creepo breather." She sashayed, hips undulating, to the bathroom.

Joey checked his Caller ID.

No name.

No need.

He knew Heather's number by heart.

Damn. He flushed at the memory of his idiotic, inexplicable confession on stage. She was the last person he wanted to talk to. He'd been half out of his mind. Fame made him crazy. Millions of people loved him. Millions of strangers.

Not that he wanted the real thing. His coming home didn't have anything to do with Heather Wade.

He'd flown home to ground himself. The press had printed so many damn lies about him, he didn't know who he was. It was as if the real Joey Fasano had ceased to exist. Posters of his tough face and body papered the world. The media made him into a sexual god, a macho warrior. But the real man felt even more invisible than he had when he'd been a nobody. When had his own life gotten so out of hand? What the hell could he do about it?

Heather. She'd called.

He felt a weird sensation inside his chest. It was as if his flesh were being flayed, sliced.

Forget her.

An uneasy stillness descended over him. He wanted to hate her, to forget her—but it wasn't that easy.

Joey sighed. Despite his own meteoric climb to fame and fortune, despite his pretense at style, he was just an actor which meant he was upstart trash in Heather's world. Her fiancé was a blue-blooded prince from old money. Joey played bad-boy outlaws that thrilled shallow, mass audiences. He didn't know squat about opera or deep literature. He couldn't stand tea parties or debutante balls.

The bathroom door opened and Daniella, having shed everything except her black, stiletto heels, swayed toward him.

Her blond hair was wild and unrestrained. She was gorgeous, and it worried him that he wasn't aroused.

He shucked his clothes and opened a drawer. Yanking out a pair of pajamas, he pulled them on. In a panic he buttoned the shirt to the neck only to realize he'd started wrong and was a button off. He leapt into bed and doused the light.

"I'm tired," he said grumpily. "So, good night." He rolled over.

She got in beside him. He stiffened when he felt her warmth oozing nearer. Then she curled her luscious body against his back, mashing her breasts against him. He lay still, his muscles strained and taut. When her fingers groped inside his pajamas, he shoved her away.

"Not tonight, babe."

"You pathetic bastard!" She jumped up. "What if I go to the tabloids and tell your fans about your…*little*… problem?"

Violence rose in him. "Go ahead." His bluff was lethally soft. "That'll be a refreshing switch from their usual fare."

He shut his eyes.

When he got up the next morning, she was gone. So were the diamonds he'd borrowed for her to wear.

Joey punched his Caller ID, and Heather's number came up again. He went to the fridge. Since he hadn't warned Cass, there was nothing in it but beer and a coffee canister. He shook the canister and found it was empty.

He slammed the door and pitched the canister into the trash. The living room with its vaulted ceilings felt empty and huge. He was glad Danny was gone even if the house felt lonelier.

Heather.

What did he keep thinking about her? She and her family had made him feel worthless. He had scripts to read, phone calls to make.

Still, he paced restlessly across the room, finally pulling out a little drawer in a table by his sofa. Inside lay a dog-eared copy of a news magazine. On the cover a handsome dark man carried a little boy on one shoulder along a golden path through a sun-dappled forest. Heather's Pulitzer-winning picture. At first glance, the man's expression was rapt. Only at second glance did one see the evil. The child's

big-eyed gaze was equally fixed. Because of that photograph, Trevor Pilot, the man in the picture, a cold-blooded
kidnapper, was in prison. The boy's father had been the
British ambassador. The kidnapping had been international
news. When the child had been found alive because of that
picture, Heather would have been honored at the White
House. But she'd run, just like she had after Ben's death.

The little boy's almost paralyzed expression sent a chill
through Joey. Heather was so good. Why had she quit?

He thrust the magazine back into the drawer and walked
out onto his porch. As he studied the dark trees along the
creek where he and Heather had played, he saw their childhood ghosts swinging on ropes. The golden-haired girl letting go, falling into the creek, water splashing all around
her skinny body like geysers.

Every summer had been a time of enchantment. Long
summer days spent lying in the sun till their skin heated
and then cold swims in the creek. Shared refreshments afterward in his hideout; shared lunches at school because he
never brought anything really good.

They'd trusted each other completely. Only she'd known
that his father beat him and how his poverty stung him,
especially the secondhand clothes and old boots that
marked him as unworthy. That's why she'd dressed so
badly—to put him at ease. When she'd told him she was
pregnant their first year in college, he'd asked her to marry
him.

His mood grew darker. He got hungrier, too, but he
couldn't drive into town for coffee, eggs or a burger unless
he was ready to answer questions about Heather.

Fame. He wasn't handling it.

He rang Cass, who said he'd shop first thing. Joey decided to watch the news while he waited. He ambled over
to the fridge, popped the top off a beer, grabbed his remote
and collapsed onto his sofa.

There was a story about a shooting spree in an Austin

mall parking lot. A jealous husband had plugged his wife's lover through a grocery sack. The reporter noted that Texas and Mexico were engulfed by a record heat wave, that temperatures had never been so high in April, that violence seemed on the rise as a result. The next story featured Senator Wade's upcoming election and his daughter's wedding.

Blood rushed in Joey's head at the sight of Heather in Larry's arms. Six years ago, Roth had put his arms around her just like that right after Ben died. Funny, her turning to Roth, Alison's old beau, that night. Funny he hadn't realized that was the exact moment he'd lost her.

Roth still had the same flawless bone structure, the same slicked-back golden hair, the same smooth way, the same frozen eyes. Maybe he looked good to her after her other crazy boyfriends. Joey didn't like the cynical droop of that carved mouth. He disliked even more the way the older man's expression hardened every time Heather said anything offbeat. If Roth was edgy, Heather was even more so.

Her smiles were strained. Her bright lipstick and rouge made her look paler. She was too thin, too reserved, almost doll-like in her utter lack of passion. She used to be a mess—but an interesting mess. Not that the conventional dress didn't flow over her slender curves. But her stylish attire and the severe knot at her nape would have suited her mother far better. The Heather he remembered was unpredictable and loved surprises. She favored loose clothes and ethnic jewelry; she wore her hair long and flowing.

This poised socialite with the tense smile and the incredible cool was a far cry from the girl with the constant grin and the tangled ringlets who'd been up to such mischief in his hideout. The Heather he'd known had wanted to experience life to its fullest, not to repress herself.

What had killed Heather's incandescent warmth and bubbly spontaneity? Why had she given up her career?

There were video shots of that antebellum mansion near

New Orleans. Suddenly an unidentified black-haired imp exploded out of the front door and hurtled off that wide veranda like a cannonball straight into Roth's waiting arms.

The little boy flashed a know-it-all grin from behind Roth's wide shoulder. Why, the kid couldn't be a day over five—

Joey shot forward on the couch.

The kid could have passed for his double at the same age. He even had that same impossible cowlick over his left temple.

Coincidence?

The next footage was of a startled Heather, who was trying to herd the child back inside away from the cameras.

A growl came out of Joey's throat. The radiance he had longed to see in her cheeks drained every drop of blood from his savage face. Flushed with embarrassment, she led the lively child away.

Had she despised him and thought him so worthless she'd lied about their baby?

Joey's mind spun back to that terrible time when Heather had fainted at Ben's funeral and been rushed to the hospital. It had been hours before Joey had gotten to see her.

Heather had lain as still as death in that curtained-off bed in that awful hospital recovery room. When Joey had walked in she'd twisted her white face away from him, but not before he'd seen the stark loss in her tear-glazed eyes. Not before he'd felt that scary emptiness inside himself.

She'd told him to go. She'd said, ''There is no baby.''

He'd gone home only to have his father beat him because Julia had run away. When Joey had staggered out of the house, Travis Wade and Larry Roth had pounced on him. They'd stuffed him into Larry's car, driven him out of town and thrown him out on the gravel shoulder. They'd roughed him up even worse than his father had, leaving marks that hadn't faded for weeks.

Semiconscious, he'd stared up at Wade, not that he could see him through the haze of blood. But he'd heard him.

"Stay away from my daughter. The last thing she wants is a lowlife like you around. If you ever come back, I'll make you sorry."

For six years Joey had been a dead man. He'd tried to fill the void inside himself with fame, money, and sex. Somehow he'd avoided drugs and some of the darker dangers so tempting to lonely creative people in his brutally competitive business. Even though he was a star, he knew what every star knows—stardom doesn't last.

What would he have when the ride was over?

He'd loved Heather. Not for her money. For who she was. All these years, Joey had lived with a hollow vacancy in his heart. When he'd gotten rich and successful, he still hadn't bothered her—other than that one phone call. Not because of her father but because *she*'d made it clear she didn't want to see him.

Joey's eyes were cold with contempt as he stared at the television set.

There is no baby.

Joey drank his beer silently, taking long swallows as he thought about Nicky.

Whose was he?

Heather was coming to Texas.

Joey decided he'd ask her.

Three

Her mother's friends from the fund-raiser would have been shocked at Heather's appearance this morning. A snarl of wiry, finger-combed, golden corkscrew curls were twisted into a lopsided ponytail that sprouted from the crown of her head and cascaded in weedy tangles over her face and ears. Gone was the gorgeous red ballgown; she now wore torn jeans with holes in the knees and a baggy football jersey. Instead of diamonds, a cross made of real nails from a month spent building a clinic in Chile dangled from a worn leather strap around her neck. Her skin was scrubbed shiny clean.

The morning was so uncustomarily hot, she wished she'd put on cutoffs. Balancing three teetering boxes on top of each other, she impatiently kneed the screen door open. She'd gone to bed at dawn and then slept through her alarm. She hadn't replaced the phone on the hook or called her mother.

"How could I have slept till noon?" Heather whined to

the ever-patient Julia who was right behind her. "Laurence and Mother probably think I'm halfway to central Texas by now. After what Joey did last night, I bet they're furious—"

"Pro-cras-ti-na-na-SHUN, Mommy!" Nicky shrieked in his favorite, earsplitting octave, pouncing on the last syllable of the new word with the relish of a little boy who could barely remember it.

"Procrastination," repeated Heather, scanning the woods out of habit. "And don't shout in your outdoor voice unless you go way, way out in the yard. Way over to that big oak tree where your tree house is."

"You want to hear a fun-fact—?" Nicky whizzed past the two women. "Squirrels are rodents. Yuck! They are cousins to rats and to mice!"

"Dear, the reason you're late," replied Julia who was juggling a load of boxes even taller than Heather's, "is because your wayward, atypical heart is not in this marriage. You haven't forgotten Joey any more than he's—"

"Would you get off that? He was a huge mistake in my life. Huge. I can't go back, and I'm not going to waste the rest of my life mooning for something that's bad for me the way you've apparently decided to—"

Julia went still. When Heather's gaze flew to the gold cross beneath Julia's crisp, white collar, she had the grace to flush with remorse. "I—"

Having lost her brother and her sister…and Joey, too, for that matter, Heather loved Julia more than most women love their most cherished friends. Julia was Joey's sister…Julia was her cherished friend. Through the darkest times of their lives, they'd had only each other. At one point, Julia had been so fragile, Heather had been terrified of losing her, too.

"You swore you weren't going to start that again," Julia began.

"Sorry."

The faint breeze wafting through the moss-laden trees sent leaves skittering across the gray planks of the veranda.

Julia's black eyes held hurt. "I'm very happy in my new vocation. You must believe that."

Julia's breathtakingly lovely face was as pure and gentle as an angel's. The thick, ebony hair she'd once worn in sexy waves was a neat glossy cap now. No spark lit the serene, black eyes that had once flashed with such devilment.

"It's so hard for me to accept you as a nun."

"Think of me as a teacher of small children...who wants to work small miracles."

"And you will. It's a miracle the way your soft voice is instantly obeyed...even in the rowdiest classroom."

"I used to be as wild as the worst of them."

"Yes." Heather smiled fondly, remembering.

Maybe having known the wilder Julia was what made it so hard to accept the newly dignified Sister Julia. *Her* Julia had climbed trees and gotten into more scrapes than Joey or Nicky. *Her* Julia had loved Ben with the same sort of wild, sexual abandon Heather had felt for Joey.

Heather and Julia had taken insane risks; they'd paid dearly, too.

"I'll go along with your choice," Heather said with gentle determination, "if you go along with mine."

"No fair. Mine's right."

"I have a son to raise. I'm tired of pretending I don't...for my father's sake. Larry will adopt him. I can claim him openly. Besides, it's time I got married and settled down."

"To a man you love, a man who loves you back. You can't live life by your father's rule book."

"Laurence and I love each other."

"No," Julia asserted sweetly, wiping her perspiring brow. "Your family loves the conventional life Laurence will give you. They didn't like Joey, or the musician, or that Arab. They want you to live the sort of life Alison would have lived—to be the pretty daughter who smiles for a few photographs when your father's campaigning, who has pretty babies, but retreats properly to the background. You're not like that.''

''From now on I will be.''

''You're sacrificing yourself again. Larry is much too old for you. The truth is that some women can only love one man. You love my brother.''

''No. You and I know the danger of that sort of love.''

Julia's luminous dark eyes flashed ruefully to Nicky who was excitedly popping the door handle of Heather's car up and down. ''Every time I look at Nicky, I see Joey. Maybe you and I made even bigger mistakes than we realized.''

Suddenly Heather saw Joey's face on that stage again, and the memory of his hard-edged, lonely, male glamor made her wince.

With some effort, Heather concentrated on the half-hearted streamers of warm sunlight that filtered through damp moss, and oak, and pine. She thrust her chin higher, marching with her boxes down the stairs of Belle Christine to her white station wagon that was parked in the dappled shade of the drive.

When she reached the car, Nicky released the handle and dived for her ankles.

''I wanna go too!''

Heather's boxes toppled out of her arms.

''Nicky, honey, watch—'' She leaned down. ''You know you want to stay with Julia—''

Nicky snatched a small box, peeling its brown flaps open. ''If you don't lemme go, I'm gonna hide this.''

Curious, he stuck his black head inside the box. Then he pulled out a yellowed picture of Joey hanging upside down on a swing.

His pudgy finger pointed. ''Me?''

Brightening with hot shame, Heather shook her head blindly.

"Who?"

"Just give it back—"

His quick, curious smile that was so like Joey's twisted her heart.

"No! Mine!"

In his quick dash to escape with his prize, Nicky's short legs tripped on a gnarled root, and he plunged forward. Cardboard flaps ripped apart. Loose photographs spewed onto lush, green grass.

Nicky popped back up, his eyes and smile devil-bright as he got to his feet in the tall grasses. The picture of Joey had torn in two. Nicky held the bottom half. Warily he dusted himself off.

"Young man—"

At her sharp tone, he bounded toward the bayou.

Every day he looked and acted more like Joey.

The air was muggy and fiercely warm. After only one trip to the car, Heather felt limp from the heat. "I wish he wouldn't go so far. I'm afraid he's going to be a handful," Heather apologized to Julia. "He's not sure about the move. He doesn't want to leave his friends."

Heather could hear Nicky moving through the ferns. She didn't like it when he got out of sight.

She sank to the ground and began cramming pictures back inside the box, hoping Julia wouldn't notice most of them were of Joey.

Julia knelt to help. "Why…you've kept all of them. These are of Joey…and Ben…and me." With a gasp she lifted a snapshot of the four of them in black leather jackets. They'd been teenagers joyriding in Ben's bright red sports car.

"That always was my favorite picture of Ben," Julia whispered, fanning herself with another picture. "And this one of me pregnant— You swore you got rid of those."

"You were so depressed, I would have said anything to protect you. I'm sorry. You know how I am about pictures. I can't bear to throw even one away."

Thankfully Julia was so absorbed in her own memories, she seemed not to notice how many shots were of Joey.

"We were so young. Ben was so happy, so alive—" Julia bit her lips. "This one of him in the cowboy hat used to be pinned to my bulletin board. I used to stare at it for hours. When I did my hair... When I talked on the phone...."

They grew silent. Images of Ben's broken red car, of his still, pale face on the rocky ground that had been bleached white in the moonlight were burned into both their minds.

Gently Heather replaced Ben's picture in the box.

"Do you hate me because for so long I couldn't bear to remember—"

"You know I don't," Heather said. "We can't change what happened."

Julia picked up the yellowed half of the one of Joey hanging upside down in the tree.

"Why does Nicky have to look so much like—"

"Maybe it's God's will," Julia said. "Maybe He doesn't want you to forget."

Heather paled when her friend's gaze fixed on her face. Joey's unspoken name hung in the stillness, invisible and yet too heavy a thing to stir in the breeze that churned the dust and leaves around their slim ankles. Unspoken memories and truths as well as the secrets they had kept charged the air between them. There had been a time when Heather had longed for Joey so much she would have gone back to him had it not been for Nicky and her fear for Julia.

"You still love him," Julia said.

Quickly Heather buried Joey's picture facedown in the box beneath Ben's.

"I see it in your expression."

"Please, Julia..."

"You can't marry Laurence. You love kids...and help-
ing people. You love all kinds of people...not just rich
blue-bloods. Larry's cold and ambitious."

"You don't know him."

"I know Joey."

"Who's hardly a saint."

"Joey's lost. The same way you are. For the same reason."

Heather was about to protest, but in the next breath, she
felt Julia's hand smooth her damp hair. The old familiar
despair that had once so terrified her came and went in her
friend's big, dark gaze.

"I'm sorry, darling," Julia said. "You've suffered so
much...and not just because of Ben. Because of me, too.
You have so much compassion for others. You sacrificed
yourself...what you felt for Joey...for the rest of us. I owe
you."

Nicky's black head peeped through the bright green fo-
liage along the brown bayou.

"We should have told Joey the truth a long time ago,"
Julia said.

"He wouldn't have left us alone. He's so famous, the
whole world would have known about us, about the baby,
about Nicky, too. The tabloids would have gone crazy, and
that would have been disastrous for my father. Not to men-
tion—*your* father."

"Maybe we should have gutted up...and stood up to our
fathers. Secrets are lies of omission. I think we made a
terrible mistake not to tell Joey," Julia said. "He would
love Nicky...so much. The same way you do."

In spite of the heat, Heather shivered. Julia's sudden
change of heart made her own burden of guilt about Joey
too heavy to endure.

No wonder the paparazzi were such a turned-on, ener-
getic bunch. Tonight's spying had given Joey a helluva

rush.

In less than an hour he'd watched a man and a woman ditch spouses, strip naked, plunge into the icy creek, and coil themselves around each other like two eels.

Sex in cold water? Even on such a hot night?

He needed to get his hands on whatever they were taking.

When the pair paddled downstream, Joey crouched lower in the dense cedar behind the boathouse. Training his binoculars on the brightly lit Wade mansion, he sucked in a sharp breath when Heather swirled into his field of vision.

Prim, pale yellow froth hugged her slim curves. Her hair was pulled up into an elegant coil. Diamonds lit her throat. One glimpse of her dynamite figure in that elegant gown, and Joey got as tense and aroused as the lustiest teenager.

The tightness of his jeans damn sure got his attention, maybe because it had been a while. Why did that trapped look and the leaden sadness in her violet eyes so rivet him? How could a bride stand in the midst of that golden window surrounded by friends and family and look so lost and alone? Where was her groom?

Why did *he* give a damn?

Someone called to her, and she vanished. But that one glimpse triggered a raw ache inside Joey that wouldn't quit. The same emptiness was in his own eyes every time he saw himself in a mirror.

His brown hands clenched the binoculars. He felt the sultry air burning his lungs every time he breathed. Her lies had put him in hell. That he felt anything for her, even lust, disgusted him. He was a fool to feel sorry for her. She was having herself a helluva party.

Because of her, he'd spent a lot of lonely years. He'd probably be messed up the rest of his life, too. Joey knew it had never occurred to her to invite him. She probably never gave him a thought. She believed her secret was safe, that she was rid of him for good.

Well, Joey wasn't leaving till he found out about her kid. If he didn't find out tonight, he'd follow her down the aisle and confront her in front of all her snooty friends tomorrow. Not that he wanted to make a fool of himself in public so soon after Oscar night. But, hell, the second time was always easier.

It was 1:00 a.m. He was dead tired. After a week of trying to contact her, he was running out of time. He had to talk to her tonight. Until he did, no way was he jumping onto his motorcycle and roaring back through the trees to his ranch house.

So, Joey studied the endless stream of guests coming and going up the drive to the party after the rehearsal dinner. Her father's guards were posted at every door. No way would they let him get close enough to talk to Heather.

Joey had tried to call her, but Travis had answered and told him to get lost. When he'd come by, Travis's men had called the sheriff.

So, tonight Joey had dug out the black leather jacket he'd worn in *Hellraiser*. Cass must've buried the thing in mothballs. The stinky jacket fit him like a second skin and had nearly a million silver zippers, most of which didn't work. Despite the heat, he'd put on the jacket for protection. Then he'd ridden over by way of overgrown, dirt-bike paths known only to him.

Shrieks of laughter blurred in the juniper-scented, night dark. The heavy beat of rock music thrummed. Dancers began to gyrate behind the long windows. Joey caught more glimpses of Heather looking sad and lost as she danced with every man except her fiancé.

For a happy couple about to be married, the bride and groom damn sure seemed to be avoiding each other.

Somewhere Joey heard a glass break. Bursts of embarrassed laughter came from the woods when the swimmers left the creek and got dressed.

Just as Joey had decided to risk edging closer to the

mansion on the chance that Heather might come out, two tall men in white dinner jackets left the house and strode quickly toward the boathouse.

One was tall, blond, magnificently tailored. His gorgeous, aristocratic mouth drooped with arrogant displeasure as he listened to his shorter, sleazier companion.

Bingo. Mr. Laurence Roth, the missing bridegroom.

The man with him was an oozier replica of Roth. Younger, thinner, the narrow, unshaven face was framed by pale, limp hair that hung in greasy strings. The smaller man's gaze brightened when Laurence slid an envelope out of his jacket.

"It's too hot to be outside," Laurence snapped.

"I got to pay somebody quick."

"This better last." Laurence held the envelope just out of reach.

"You like me to beg—"

"Just a friendly warning."

"Things happen."

"You make it happen, Oscar."

Oscar leapt for the envelope and grabbed it as ferociously as a dog might seize a bone.

"A thank-you would be nice," Roth said.

Oscar snorted. "What's a brother for?"

"That's what I'd like to know."

An awkward moment passed. "Okay. I owe you."

"Take a nice long trip."

"Maybe I want to see you walk down the aisle?"

"No!"

"Have you even told *her* about me?"

"She thinks I'm noble to help you."

"So—is she as hot in the sack as your usual babes?"

Joey's eyes narrowed. *Damn the jerk.*

"She's a senator's daughter. Her father can open doors."

"So, you two haven't done it yet," Oscar sneered.

"I'm sorry we're having this conversation."

"I got just the thing to make her forget that macho actor—'' Oscar's hand dug in a back trouser pocket.

Joey went wild inside when he saw a slender blonde in frothy yellow step onto the terrace with a drink in one hand and a bouquet of yellow roses in the other.

Oh, God. No.

Still, just the sight of her lit a match to Joey's flesh.

Worriedly Heather scanned the darkness. "Larry—''

"Down here, darling." Laurence glared at Oscar. "Scram!"

"Not till I pop this little sucker into her drink."

"You swore you were clean." Laurence swiped his brother's hand aside in disgust.

Joey sucked in a tight breath. He'd heard about monsters in bars who put exotic drugs into women's drinks to make them helpless.

Heather joined the two men in the boathouse.

"You remember Oscar, darling?"

She was as warm and effusive as Larry was cool. "Your brother," she gushed.

"Oscar's got a plane to catch. It's too hot to stay out here."

"But—''

Absently she set her drink on the railing. Quick as a flash Oscar's hand swept across her glass.

Bastard.

When Heather lifted her drink again and drained the contents, Oscar grinned. "You two have fun, big brother. And…thanks."

As the band began to play, Oscar vanished into the dark, and Laurence slipped an arm around Heather. "I'm sorry I got so bent out of shape about that damned Joey Whats-His-Name."

"You know his name…Fasano." She paused.

Roth stiffened.

"I know it's a little warm, but would you dance with me?" she whispered.

"I thought you'd never ask."

They went into one another's arms awkwardly and began dancing. Within seconds her head fell back against his shoulder.

"Maybe it's the heat.... I feel so weak—" Her voice was faint, strange, breathy. Yellow roses tumbled one by one from her fingers.

Laurence lifted her chin and began to kiss her.

Joey scowled. Then he swallowed a deep lungful of pungent night air laced with the cloying scent of cedar and almost choked on the murderous breath.

"My lovely, lovely Heather," Laurence whispered, nibbling her ear. When he deepened his kisses, Heather clung.

Soon, the action was so hot and heavy Joey lowered his face in disgust. The leather jacket made him feel like he was boiling alive.

Damn.

When Joey looked up, her hair had come loose. The bouquet of yellow roses lay crushed beneath Larry's heel in the dirt. Heather was trying to twist away from Laurence. Instead of letting her go, Laurence pushed her up against a column and slid a forceful knee between her legs. Her long neck fell back. When she struggled to lift her head, she couldn't. "No...no," she whispered woozily.

She said no, you bastard.

"Heather.... You've made me wait too long. Now everybody's laughing at me because of that movie star. You've got to let me. You've got to prove you love me, not him."

She pushed at Roth. "No.... I feel...hot.... Sick. Not right."

She resisted but more weakly. Laurence's ardor grew. When she tried to twist free, she stumbled on a loose flagstone step.

Then she couldn't stand, and Laurence knelt and lifted her. Dizzily she collapsed, and he gathered her into his arms.

"Let me help you." Laurence's voice soothed, infinitely tender.

Her head lolled back, her golden hair streaming against his shoulder. Low, tortured sounds escaped her throat as if she were now only semiconscious.

"I want to lie down," she whispered as Laurence headed toward the woods.

A bomb ticked inside Joey in a deadly countdown.

"Of course, darling." Laurence's lip curled.

She said no.

A dark, primal rage rose up in Joey as he sprang from the trees and stalked them as swiftly as a panther.

Four

Something was wrong.

Weird black shapes mushroomed in size and swirled around Heather like lurid devils.

The drink.

But she'd only had one, and she'd danced for hours. So, how could she feel roaring drunk? She'd never been drunk in her life.

Her stomach ached. Her nerves tingled. She felt lighter than air. At the same time she felt all silken and strange and warm and heavy inside.

She was sprawled across a lumpy bed in the guest cottage. No, she was on a chenille cloud, floating. Vaguely she was aware of a huge weight toppling across her, of a man's strong legs anchoring her, of hands digging into her and pressing her down, of a knee forcing her thighs apart.

With the greatest effort she willed herself to open her eyelids. Briefly she saw Laurence's golden head at her throat. He was breathing heavily, his lips sucking at her like a leech. His large hands were all over her, groping.

What was wrong with him? What was wrong with her? She didn't want this. Laurence was a gentleman. Why wouldn't he listen to her?

"No.... No...." she whispered. Why wouldn't he stop?

"No...." The soundless cry vibrated inside her.

Maybe he wasn't listening because he couldn't hear her. She fought to scream harder.

"No...."

Her lips formed the word, mouthed it, but no sound came out. It was as if her tongue was frozen, her throat numb.

Her heart beat at triple speed, and yet her muscles felt paralyzed. She was limp and relaxed; and utterly terrified.

What was wrong with her?

"I can't wait," he whispered.

His hands yanked at the zipper of her dress. When it gave, and she felt cotton peeling and tearing away from her body, she tried to scream.

Again, only plaintive, indistinct gurgles came out. Frantic, she fought harder.

"No—"

This time the sound she made bordered on a sob.

Still, he didn't stop.

Tears streamed down her cheeks when he jerked the gown over her hips and tossed it to the floor.

She willed herself to fight harder, but it was as if she were a statue. Slowly the rafters above Laurence's dark face blurred. As he lowered himself over her, she realized there was nothing she could do to stop him.

She was utterly helpless, and all alone.

She wanted to weep, to die.

All was lost.

She went numb, inside and out.

It didn't matter what happened to her.

Nothing mattered.

She was drifting, floating away from him. Under the influence of the drug, her mind, which could form erratic images in the best of times, began to hallucinate. Laurence took the shape of a dragon with seven heads whose flaming tongues burned her to a heap of ash. Next he was a huge black octopus, dragging her into the inky deep. Her skull banged against the headboard, and she realized that it was Larry and not some monster after all.

Panicking as blackness closed over her, she screamed.

Somewhere a door opened, and cool night air gusted against her bare skin. The strange odor of mothballs and old leather snapped her back to consciousness.

"Get off her." The raspy snarl penetrated even her drugged state. "Get off her, you bastard, or I'll kill you."

"You're that damned creep, Fasano—the movie star! She's *my* girl now, you son-of-a—"

Joey's gaze burned through to her soul.

Joey. Oh, thank God. It was Joey.

Her eyes filled with tears of gratitude as Laurence was yanked off her, and she could breathe again. Dazedly she watched as the two of them scuffled on the floor.

Furniture scraped harshly as they rolled over, kicking and cursing each other.

Joey's fist rose and crashed into Laurence's jaw, and Laurence went down hard, groaning and writhing.

As Joey strode toward her, Laurence became some sort of reptile whose tail thrashed back and forth, in agony now.

The mattress dipped when Joey knelt beside her.

"Heather."

Joey's gorgeous mouth thinned in stern disapproval. She forced herself to forget that reptilian tail and focus on Joey's hard face, especially on the shape of his long, narrow nose, on his nostrils flaring in anger. She puckered her nose at the reek of odors she associated with old wool stored too long in cedar closets.

The dear face blurred. She stared up at him blankly. Through him.

She tried to speak, but her breath stalled.

"Oh, Joey."

Instead of his name, all that came out was a whimper.

A helpless tear trickled down her cheek.

She felt nothing.

He seemed to understand. When she began to shiver and her teeth to chatter, he pulled her close and held her against his muscular chest, rocking her back and forth, his body heat seeping inside her.

"There, there. You've had a bad scare. You're gonna be okay."

Gently, with his callused hand, he soothingly brushed the cascade of hot tears from her icy cheeks. With equal care, he eased his black jacket off his powerful shoulders and slipped her trembling body into it. Then, as if she weighed no more than a kitten, he lifted her into his powerful arms and carried her out into the velvet dark, the forest of their childhood, that smelled sweetly of juniper and wildflowers.

Carefully he placed her in front of him on his motorcycle. Then he straddled the seat and stomped down hard on something until the huge engine roared to life, its vibrations making her body shake and come alive again.

It was the most wonderful sound she'd ever heard.

Wrapped in his hard arms, and held against his long, male length, she began to feel safe.

For years she'd told herself she'd been weak and bad to love him; the drug stripped away that shame. She knew only a mindless glory to be who she really was, to be Joey's girl again.

"Close your eyes," he ordered.

Then he tore away with her through the deep black trees over rough trails with her long gold hair streaming away from her face against his wide shoulders.

* * *

Heather was safe now. Or at least she felt warm and cozy, like a butterfly in a snug cocoon. Somewhere an air conditioner hummed, sending drafts of cool air into what had been an airless room.

They were in some deserted cabin on his ranch. What had Joey said? That he used it for hunting sometimes or that he came here when he wanted to be alone to study for a part? He'd stripped his jacket off her and left it on the porch. To air out, he'd whispered with a conspiratorial smile as he'd wrapped her in a blanket.

She couldn't remember much else of what he'd said or done, but she could open her eyes again. Her lids no longer felt like burning, leaden weights over her eyes. And through the dirty panes of a window, she could see a ripe, overlarge moon hanging like a bleached silver disc above the tops of the trees.

Where was she?

Where she wanted to be, she mused dreamily, like a princess in a fairy tale under a spell.

Where she'd always wanted to be.

In a soft, warm bed.

With Joey.

What her parents wanted didn't matter. What *she* really felt was finally acceptable to her. All guilt and shame were gone.

Because he had saved her.

But when she reached toward him to trace his tanned cheek with gentle, loving fingertips, his black eyes flew open and held hers, measuring her, warning her not to go so far.

Why was he so tense? What was wrong? Her brain was still fuzzy, so she didn't understand his glowering scowl of rejection.

Not that he could look away from her any more than she could look away from him. Thus, they lay perfectly still, wrapped in blankets, facing each other. For what seemed an eternity in that surreal moonlight, their adoring gazes remained joined, devouring each other's faces, relearning each feature, memorizing even the tiniest changes.

She had dated other people and tried to forget him.

For years, because of her guilt, she had lied to herself and said she had forgotten him. She had had lied to her parents, Julia, and Laurence. And by omission to Nicky.

As she studied the lean, harsh angles of Joey's dangerously masculine face, she saw how much he had suffered.

Because of her.

She longed to tell him, to show him that he had never been far from her thoughts. She longed to run her hands through his hair, to play with his stubborn cowlick as she had as a girl.

Heather didn't know that she was dreaming because her forbidden dream felt as familiar as a favorite room. Because it was. She had dreamed this very same dream every night when she'd fallen asleep. Asleep, her guilt would vanish and her mind would fill with images that held only him. And every morning she would awaken without the slightest memory of him.

At last he closed his eyes. When he began to exhale deep, even breaths, she thought he was asleep and that she could safely kiss him.

"I love you," she whispered, her low voice charged with tenderness as she traced her lips across his thick, black, feathery brow. "I always have. And I always will."

His eyes snapped open the exact moment she fell asleep. Stunned by her loveliness on his moon-washed bed, his heart thudded with raw, unwanted emotion. He should get up. Instead, he lay beside her for what seemed like hours, watching her with a raptor's unblinking, predatory gaze.

Unsmiling, he observed her full-lipped mouth, the sensuous curl of her long, spiked lashes and hated that just looking at her made him breathless.

She was so damned beautiful. She'd made him feel so

worthless, he'd been driven to insane heights to prove he was worthy. And what had he proved—that he was still a fool when it came to Heather Wade?

After tonight he wondered if he'd ever be able to put her out of his mind. Slowly, very slowly, her nearness and warmth lulled him into drowsiness, and he drifted off, too.

Joey hadn't known he was asleep, until her low seductive moan startled him into wakefulness again. If possible the moon was brighter, fuller, diffusing the cabin with its soft, white light.

She had moved closer to him. Before he could edge away, he felt her slim, warm hand inside the waistband of his jeans. Her shy fingertips pocketed against his flesh electrified him.

After months of not wanting any woman, his libido roared into overdrive. Instantly he was as hot and hard as a loaf of bread fresh out of an oven.

Her power to arouse him terrified him. Sensing his weakness, she squirmed nearer, her soft warm female flesh smelling sweetly of soap and juniper. With a faint smile, she nestled into him.

She was heaven. Pure bliss.

No.

The bliss had gone out of his young life one tragic night.

If he was going to talk to her, he had to wait this special brand of torment out, regain control—

Her hands fumbled inside his jeans. "Joey," she breathed, stroking him in her sleep.

He was supposed to be the brazen one.

"Joey—" Her soft, velvety voice held wonder, adoration, familiarity; her urgent fingers made him ache.

Not with her. Never again.

Six years ago she'd condemned him to a lonely hell. He wanted to feel nothing for her.

She was drugged out of her mind.

The honorable thing was to protect her till she came to her senses.

Get real. You don't have an honorable bone in your body, Fasano. Neither does she.

She deserves the worst. So, do it.

He thought of their first time together. They'd been necking in his Chevy, the pink roses he'd stolen out of her mother's garden laying askew on the dashboard of the car. His hands had been entwined in the masses of her golden hair. Jeans off, their perspiring bodies were glued together that long summer night. He'd been every bit as scared as she was, but he'd said cockily, "The first time, you should do it with someone good, someone who knows how."

"You think you know so much about girls and sex, but you don't know anything, Fasano. A girl would rather do it with the boy she loves."

"I love you then," he'd quickly agreed, little realizing how deeply he'd meant it.

Love. He hated that meaningless buzzword for the self-destructive emotion he was determined never to feel for any woman—especially her—again.

"You'd say anything right now," the teenage Heather had teased, seizing a rose and brushing the tip of his nose with it.

"But I do love you," he'd proclaimed recklessly. "I do."

The woman beside him smelled of roses, too—as the girl had that first night.

Forget the past. Forget love.

"Stay away from me," he rasped, clamping his fist around her wrist. "You'll take your hands off me...if you know what's good for you."

Her fingers tightened.

"Heather," he gasped. "Oh, God, Heather, honey— Don't do that— Please—" He sucked in an agonized breath.

"I love you," she whispered. "I want you. Only you—"

Love. The word ate at him like acid. Six years of heartbreak rushed back—the long lonely nights spent in trailers in jungle locations. The years of being mobbed by strangers and yet not having a friend on the set to so much as share a beer with or to confide in.

His fame had cut him off from everyone.

Heather's golden hair shimmered like skeins of silk in the moonlight. Her beautiful face was stark white; her violet eyes glittered with desperate emotions as dark and needy as his own.

"You're not the only one who's been unhappy, Joey...or lonely. I wanted to forget you, too."

When he tried to push her away, she put a soft hand to his face, stroking his cheek with feather-light fingertips. "You want to hate me, right...because I broke up with you? But it doesn't have to be that way." She flipped her hand and brushed the bridge of his nose with her knuckles, the way she'd done when she'd been his girl.

Her fingertips were scented with roses. "If you don't like what happened between us, maybe our story isn't finished. Maybe you should do something about it, rewrite our ending."

He held his breath, considering her words, in spite of everything.

She'd been his first woman. His only love.

No. There had been the baby, that wild night ride, Ben's broken red car, her shutting him out after Larry led her away and her family had closed ranks. There was Nicky now. Roth, too. And other hurts.

If they hadn't loved, Ben wouldn't have died. If she hadn't been ashamed of being pregnant by a Fasano, they wouldn't have sent Ben off on that wild, midnight ride. If...if...if....

He hated her for the emptiness and dissatisfaction he'd

found in all his relationships with the girlfriends who had followed her.

Heather had been born rich, to a politician. Politics made liars out of everyone, especially their families. Or maybe it was just the money that had robbed her of a real heart. Money was a kind of anesthesia that made the world and other people's pain feel less real.

Her parents had taught her to be a snob and hypocrite. They'd spoiled her. She'd been given everything while he'd had to scrabble his way from out of the gutter to get to the top.

Ben was dead. Joey couldn't change the part he'd played in that tragedy. All he wanted now was to find out about their baby.... About that rowdy, black-haired little boy.

She leaned closer and pressed her mouth to Joey's. One taste was like a whiff of an addictive drug. His black lashes lowered, her eagerness luring him closer to that dangerous high.

Again he remembered that first night when he'd made love to her. The moon had been huge, magical like this one. The air had been scented with roses, and she had been bathed in ashy, white light as she was now.

"Joey, don't hate me." She crushed her mouth to his as if to savor the man he'd become. His body quaked, hardened, cramped, rebelled. The past that had haunted him, the past that should have separated them—bound him to her instead. He remembered all the good times they'd shared.

One magic afternoon they'd made love on top of the dam with the sunlight filtering through the brightly-lit, emerald canopy of the trees overhead, with the cold water swirling around them. He'd stared up at those flickering leaves and let her ride him. He remembered another glorious time in the woods when he'd held her against that cypress trunk and she'd wrapped her legs around his waist and held on. When he'd exploded, the air around them had exploded too—with bursts of orange monarch butterflies. Then he remembered the nights in his hideout where they'd lain on blankets in the dark and he'd pointed out the constellations.

Her trembling lips brought a tide of bittersweet memories. Soon, he could barely manage even token resistance.

A fierce tremor swept him as her lips lingered burningly. When the tip of her pink tongue teased his mouth apart, his heart pumped wildly. On a long shudder, he pulled her tighter.

Sensing how near he was to surrender, her low, thick whisper caught him by surprise. "You used to tempt me. It's my turn tonight. I'm going to make you want me again and love me again, Fasano. And this time, you'll never let me go."

Love?

No way, babe. The most glamorous women in the world throw themselves at me day and night. I can't even get it up.

No way will I fall for you again.

His eyes snapped open. His scowl dark and fierce. She'd thrown him out and made him feel worse than the lowest worm.

Heather dazzled him with a smile.

There were marks on her neck, cruel bruises. The bastard had hurt her. The depth of his concern stunned Joey as he brushed his palm along the dark marks.

A firestorm of emotion whirled around him and took charge, making mockery of his hatred. Her nearness, her scent, her touch, her seeking lips, her vulnerability, all aroused him to near bursting.

Some men never learn. Love doesn't always come in neat packages with declarations and vows. It steals with equal ease into fierce, unwilling hearts.

She had already seized him by storm.

Get the hell up, Fasano.

Run.

Take a hike in the woods.

Wash yourself down with icy creek water.

Heather's soft gaze was hot and full of mischief. It caught him off guard with wild, erotic promises and melted his resolve.

No way could he leave her when she was drugged, he rationalized. She might do herself some harm while he was gone. He had no choice but to protect her.

With her mouth, she traced a scorching trail down the length of his torso, leaving the skin on his flat belly tingly with aftershocks.

He lay as still as an enchanted statue beneath her, his heart thudding, his control ebbing. It was as if she were a sensual witch who'd cast a spell, as if she held him prisoner to her every whim and captive to his own desire. With her hands and her mouth she shaped his unwilling flesh into living, molten stone.

When her trembling hands unzipped his jeans and tugged them off, he stared fixedly at the ceiling. Next her heated fingertips were on his bare behind, sliding his shorts down his legs. When he didn't try to undress her, she stood over him. Like a stripper, who was both innocent and bold, she toyed with a spaghetti strap of her pale yellow slip, hesitating for a suspenseful moment before pushing it off her shoulder. With a look of surprise, she touched the second strap. When it fell too, she got on the bed and crawled toward him on her knees, her breasts bouncing, so that the fragile silk slid to their tips.

He shut his eyes. But that was the most dangerous thing he could do. Her image burned brightly behind his closed eyelids, even more magnificent in his imagination. When he opened his eyes again, her silk slip was bunched at her waist.

He caught his breath as she pushed the fragile garment lower. When she peeled the thing down her thighs and then completely off, his eyes darkened.

Bathed in the silver glow of the moonlight, she licked

her lips before lowering her golden head to his groin. He held his breath as her head dipped, her silken hair swishing his legs. Her warm breath sent fiery pinpricks everywhere.

"Heather..." he accused hoarsely. "You threw me out. You damn near destroyed me."

"It was hard for me, too. You'll never know how hard. I looked for love in all the wrong places. I made so many stupid mistakes."

"Tell me about it, babe."

"I'm sorry. So sorry for everything. I never got over you, Joey. That's the truth. I never will."

She continued loving him. Desire saturated his mind, his body. He had to stop her.

His heart roared in his ears. His harsh indrawn breath almost strangled him as he arched himself deeply toward her parted lips.

With her moist tongue she made love to every long delicious, corded inch of him. With each silken flick, with each little whimper, his heartbeats quickened till he thought he would explode.

His hard-muscled body was beaded in perspiration when she finally lifted her glassy, amethyst gaze to his.

Push her away. Resist.

She rose to a half crouch and spread her thighs over his and sank down, down, till she sheathed him.

Blood swelled inside him as he lay beneath their bodies fused. She felt sleek and hot, deliciously wild. Her silky hair showered over her shoulders like white fire. He cupped the cheeks of her buttocks with his palms and ground himself into her.

When she laughed, he grabbed her hair, wrapped it around his fist, and pulled her face down to his. Closing his eyes, he kissed her with savage, practiced mastery. Only he wasn't acting. She was real. His need was real.

"I missed you, Joey. I missed this." Shamelessly, she dug her hands into his shoulders as he began to rock them.

She was as tight as a glove. As wild as a wanton. She had him at her mercy. He told himself to enjoy her now, that there would be time enough to hate her afterward.

"You've had all those women," she moaned as the mattress bounced.

His body stilled; his mouth tensed.

"I—I haven't had anyone...since you," she confessed in a muffled, tragic tone.

"What about all those other guys?"

"I didn't sleep with any of them."

Something inside him stopped dead at the sorrow in her voice.

Don't believe her. Don't let her know what that means to you.

But her eyes were so wet and luminous, he couldn't tear his gaze away. Nor his heart. With that single broken phrase she stole back his soul.

I haven't had anyone...since you.

Everything about her was both totally familiar and absolutely alien. When he had known her before she had lacked this honesty, this woman's wisdom and knowledge, this mature, voluptuous beauty, this neediness that came from long years of loneliness.

His hard arms gentled. Still, he fought the fierce pleasure.

For six years she had been his tormentor.

He hated that only she could offer him solace.

Why was it that only with her could sex consume him? Why was it that she who had made him feel worthless, could make him feel whole?

His tongue nudged inside her mouth, filled her, devoured her. On a strangled curse, Joey rolled them both over, so that his powerful body was on top of hers.

Still sheathed so warmly inside her, time dissolved as he rode her. Everything was as it had been when they were kids. When he'd loved her and butterflies had soared. When she'd given herself to him so trustingly, promising she was his forever.

Her tongue thrust inside his lips. Her fingers gripped handfuls of his long, black hair. Her legs wrapped around him. He drove into her fiercely, repeatedly, until she screamed and he exploded, spilling liquid heat inside her, losing more of himself than he knew.

Afterwards she clung, holding his damp head close so that their feverish brows touched, both of them breathing in hard and sighing softly. She murmured all those hatefully tender love words he couldn't bear to hear and yet wanted to hear more than anything. Finally, mercifully, she lapsed into silence, kissing his neck, his temples, his closed eyelids.

He lay in the dark, savoring her sweetness, wanting to hold her forever, not wanting to consider how different everything would feel in the morning.

She'd be the senator's daughter again. He'd be the vulgar movie star who'd caused her brother's death. She'd be the woman he hated. He'd be the son of her father's hated rival.

For now the silver-tinted night was scented with the magic of lovemaking and pink roses. He could hear the creek and the wind in the trees. He felt young and new. He wanted to carve their names in every tree trunk, to get in his truck and drive fast the way they'd done as kids, to brake at the last minute, to close his eyes and kiss her at every red light.

He'd never gotten over her.

He closed his eyes. In the dark his lips found hers. They made love again. Only this time he was the beggar who went down on his knees and crawled to her.

He was both sweeter and wilder. He went longer, leading her up to titillating peaks time and again, until she was quivering and desperate. Afterwards, he knew this one night would never be enough. He wanted more.

And the more he got, the more he would crave.

He was doomed.

She'd hooked him—body and soul.

Five

"Travis! Heather's gone!"

Travis shrank lower behind his *Wall Street Journal.*

When he made no answer, Nellie broke one of Travis's sacred rules and burst into his office without knocking.

Did Nellie really have to stand over him, pestering him with all this wedding madness when he had his election to worry about?

Not that Travis didn't adore her. Hell, he'd wanted her ever since she'd been sixteen and in love with that no-good Deo Fasano.

Travis had been swimming underwater in the creek. Nellie had jumped from the rope swing. When she hit the water, her bikini top had come off. At the sight of her breasts, Travis's goggles had steamed. He'd fallen instantly, irrationally, irrevocably in love.

Travis still resented how hard he'd had to fight to win Nellie from Fasano. He'd hate the name Fasano till the day he died. At fifty, Nellie was prettier than ever, thanks to diet, exercise, and a fortune on plastic surgery. Who cared if she cost plenty? She made him happy. She knew how to flatter him; she ran their domestic life smoothly; and she was a political asset. But best of all, she was as full of imaginative tricks as Houdini in their bedroom. Sex got better and better, if only on Sundays.

"Travis!"

He flipped a page.

"Hell-ooo?" Nellie's bright eyes all but burned a hole in his paper. "Our phone's ringing off the wall. We're expecting hundreds of guests. Heather's gone. And you can sit there—"

He lowered his paper. Her plump bosom swelling with indignation made him remember she'd been too busy last Sunday for their romp.

"Heather's bed hasn't been slept in!"

"Neither has ours," he retorted grumpily.

"Maybe Larry knows something—" Before Travis could stop her, Nellie had dialed the guest cottage.

At her horrified gasp, Travis snapped his paper shut.

Nellie stared at her husband. "He hung up."

Within seconds, their doorbell buzzed. Larry was on their porch, an ice pack pressed against a swollen, black eye. From the way he grimaced as he danced from one foot to the other, the man looked like he could do with a bag of ice on his testicles, too.

"Where's Heather?" Travis roared when he opened the door.

"*He* took her."

Maybe it was the hot air gusting through the cracked door that swept Travis's sanity away on a tidal wave of rage.

"Mr. Wade, it was dark. One minute I was kissing her in the boathouse. Then that cheap movie star slugged me." Laurence blurred in a hot red haze.

"Fasano! I knew when he started buying up my town that he'd be trouble."

"Travis! You're purple! Your blood pressure!"

"We're going after Fasano." Travis dug for his car keys in his pocket. "Nellie, you have to talk some sense into that crazy daughter of *yours* before she screws all our lives up again."

Heather's head throbbed. Her muscles and joints, even her bones felt achy. Her skin burned as if she had a fever. Yet, when she stirred sleepily, her body tangled in white cotton sheets and downy pillows, a gentle smile broke across her face.

Then her stomach growled. She was starving.

Mother had promised to cook eggs Benedict for her and Laurence this morning, to serve it on the terrace overlooking the creek.

Heather's long black lashes quivered when squares of bright white, as harsh and hot as strobe lights, flickered across her face. Cautiously she opened her eyes.

When she saw gray, unpainted walls instead of her own familiar wallpaper with its tiny yellow roses and pink swirls of ribbon, she blinked jerkily.

She was in a cabin. Through grimy, dirt-crusted windows she saw green trees and golden sunlight. A mourning dove cooed, forming a chorus with buzzing cicadas.

What? How? Where—

Panic thudded through her, quickening her breaths and sharpening her heartbeats.

Dimly she remembered walking onto the terrace last night, sick because Laurence had been so jealous and furious about Joey. She'd called out to Laurence in that soft, moonlit darkness. He had answered. She had run lightly down to the boathouse.

The rest of the night was a terrifying blur.

Somebody had been with Laurence. Another man. Oscar,

his brother. There had been music. She and Laurence had danced, kissed. She had gotten too warm, become dizzy.

Vague disturbing images of Laurence's wet mouth hungrily devouring hers, of Laurence carrying her somewhere into a frightening, misty void.

And then—nothing.

Absolutely nothing.

Gooseflesh pricked her skin. With an uneasy shudder, she rubbed her arms and opened her eyes wider. She must've had a bad dream.

The unvarnished rafters, walls, and dirty windows that came into sharper focus were no dream.

Where—

Outside a man hummed raspily. "—they don't know what love is—"

Startled, her gaze jerked toward the window. She sat up in a tense half crouch.

"—you can take your clothes off—"

While singing, Joey Fasano was leaning back as far as was humanly possible in a chair whose legs looked far too spindly to hold his huge, muscular body. Nevertheless, he looked as maddeningly nonchalant, as cockily unconcerned as she felt uptight and terrified.

She cringed with fresh humiliation as he droned on about each garment the woman in his song could remove and how she should do so. Mesmerized, Heather watched his brown fingers tapping out the beat of the song on his denim thigh.

Tears sprang to her eyes. Her nails dug into the cotton sheets as she scooted to the other side of the bed to get as far away from him as possible.

The springs groaned.

Bed—

She was in...in *his* bed.

The cotton sheets smelled of man. Of lovemaking. Of Joey.

There had to be a mistake.

She blinked rapidly as if that would make the nightmare dissolve. But as she peered out the window again, instead of vanishing, Joey loomed larger. With the sunlight back-lighting his ebony hair and massive shoulders, he looked even sexier than before. His upper arms bulged. He obviously took time to work out. His pectorals were well defined, his waist narrow, his abdomen as flat as a washboard. Dressed all in black, his dangerous, chiseled face with that white, devil-may-care grin had the same devastating effect it always had on her idiotic, female senses.

Joey had been born knowing more about women than most men learned in a lifetime. At least he knew about her. Doubtless, he'd used his fame and career, and all those tabloid beauties, to hone the evil tricks that came so naturally to him.

Had he seduced her?

She would kill him.

Her parents would kill her.

The urge to run away was overpowering. Somehow she had to get out of here, away from him. Somehow she had to keep her parents and Larry from finding out about this. But when she scanned the room for some means of escape, she saw that Joey Fasano had planted himself squarely in front of the only door.

She was his prisoner.

When she sat up, cool sheets sifted down her warm satin skin to reveal pert, beaded nipples.

She was naked. In *his* bed.

Knowing Joey was within half a mile, such a fact shouldn't be a big surprise. Unbidden came the memory of a torrid love scene from his most recent movie, *Bandido*. He had lassoed a girl and made love to her in a cave.

With a smothered scream, Heather yanked the covers to her throat.

Her clothes— What had he—

Shreds of yellow cotton froth hung neatly from a nearby

chair. Her stomach flipped queasily at the thought of him ripping her dress off. When her gaze leapt to her neatly folded silk slip, lacy bra and panties, her headache began to burn behind her eyelids.

Where were her shoes?

Shoes?! Focus! An irrelevant detail like shoes didn't matter. Joey Fasano had blown her carefully planned life to bits—again.

Oh, God. When she licked her lips, they felt raw and bruised. Other parts of her body were sticky and tender, too.

The sex-crazed brute.

Had she?

Shame sent a burning flush up her throat and scalded her cheeks.

What had *he* done to her?

Oh, she knew.

Heather felt like a slut.

In the next instant a fist full of brown knuckles rapped on the window pane beside the bed. "You up yet, darlin'?"

Her gaze darted toward the grimy window. Their eyes clashed through a gray streak of dirt.

She turned white and screamed.

He laughed with a boldness that sent thrilling chills down her quickly-stiffening, indignant spine.

"I'm coming in—" This raspy pronouncement sliced what was left of her fraying nerves with razor-sharp precision.

Again she screamed. Then she buried herself under the sheets and covers like a frightened child.

Her imagination went wild. She was in an ancient dungeon, chained to a dank, stone wall. He was a bold Scottish knight who'd captured her and used her sorely. Her father would send a passel of knights to skewer Joey.

The door groaned on its hinges. When Joey's custom-made, sharkskin boots stomped across the wooden threshold, she cried out, "No! Wait— Don't—"

Curiosity drove her to peek at him through a hole in his blanket. Her heart thudded and then skidded to a halt. He was so huge, his ebony head nearly grazed the rafters. His legs in skin-tight black denim were spread widely apart, his stance that of a conqueror. How could he dwarf the cabin and make her feel even tinier and more helpless than she already did?

The reality of his masculine strength and physical superiority hit her like a body blow.

"Don't be such a little coward. Come out from under that sheet."

"I'm not dressed!"

"After last night, you've got nothing to hide."

His smile and the cocky, low-throated chuckle that accompanied it were so erotic, her breath stopped in her throat.

"At least not from me," he finished, laughing.

Heather swallowed hard.

When he started swiftly toward her, the sound of his heels striking the oak planks seemed to magnify the quickness of her own hollow heartbeats. Sure he would yank the cover off or do something even worse, she held the blanket over her head and kicked…just in case he came near.

But he stood back, and laughed at her antics as if she were a child throwing a tantrum. Patiently he waited for her to exhaust herself. And soon she became so breathless and sweaty from kicking that she did have to stop.

Under the covers, the air was suddenly so dense and warm, she could barely breathe.

"It's past noon, princess."

"I'm never coming out. I'd die of shame."

"Embarrassment never killed anybody."

Little did he know. She remembered her pregnancy.

Ben's death. Her profound guilt and shame. Nicky. Her secret son had been a constant threat to her father's career.

She'd sworn she would never hurt her parents again.

Heather felt Joey's hand, gently easing the blanket away from her flushed face. She fought him still, but he was stronger and more determined.

When had she ever been able to stop Joey from having his way? He didn't stop pulling until the top of her golden head and her long-lashed, violet eyes were revealed to him.

His broad-shouldered form leaned toward her. Why did he have to be so big? His smoldering black gaze was so mortifyingly intimate that whatever doubts she had clung to about how the two of them might have passed the night together in some innocent fashion like playing cards or stealing old ladies' underwear on a dare vanished like a puff of smoke.

His heated male stare branded her his possession, his woman. His alone.

Oh, dear God. What made her so weak, so spinelessly shameful?

Why did his nearness and his exasperated, soul-weary sigh make her so dizzily breathless?

He didn't stop looking at her till he had her pale skin burning like fire.

"Does that blush go all over, honey?" His grin was too conceited for words. "Let me see."

He yanked at her blanket, but gently, just to tease her. She held on as ferociously as a determined puppy playing tug-of-war.

"You're in a different mood this morning, my pet," he said.

"I'm not your pet...."

His eyes watched her. There was something in them, some new awareness, an eagerness, that she didn't want to acknowledge.

"Last night...you were most...affectionate."

She stared at him with growing horror, her throat tight, her mouth dry. "I—I hate you."

"You couldn't get enough of me last night. You were...we were...well, pretty incredible."

Her gut twisted with fresh shame. "I don't believe you."

"I was afraid things would look different to you in the morning. You were so sweet, and so damned pretty."

"I don't believe anything you say!"

"Fine. Suit yourself." He chuckled, but her words had wiped that tender eagerness from his gaze. "Your head hurts, I'll bet. You probably don't remember much.... Lucky for you, I remember everything. So, if you get curious, I could describe our night together in the most vivid detail. In fact I'd love to do so."

Naturally, some part of her *was* avidly curious to know every sordid fact about their latest escapade. But she said, "Spare me."

His black eyes sparked. "You're sure?" As always, he could read her mind and used that knowledge to devil her. "If I don't tell you now, while it's fresh on my mind, I might forget something. You are the most incredibly sexual creature! I haven't met your equal in six years."

He dared to compare *her* to the legions of trashy women he'd bedded.

With a moan, she clamped her hands over her ears. "I am living in a nightmare."

His smile died. "So am I." With a low curse, he leaned down and jerked her toward him. "Do you think I wanted this to happen?"

In outraged modesty, she struggled against him. "I-I want to know what's going on. Why am I here?"

"You tell me."

"You thanked me Oscar night—"

A muscle clenched in his carved jawline. "Oh, that," he said. His dismissive, black gaze moved jerkily over her pink face. "Sorry. Chalk it up to stage fright."

She sensed he wasn't being entirely truthful. "You're not telling me everything—"

"Neither are you. You have a little boy— Nicky."

She went still. Staring up at him, her heart began to knock.

"He's five. His hair is black. Like mine. In fact, he bears a rather startling resemblance to me. Whose is he?"

"Mine," she breathed.

"And?"

"Please, don't," she whispered. "You have no right—"

Joey stared, his expression blank. Then his nostrils flared. The olive tint of his skin deepened. "You told me our baby died."

The blood drained from her face. Her mind spun backward to that terrible time when Ben had died and she'd lain in that hospital bed sick and brokenhearted. All she'd wanted was to do one thing right, to make her family happy and whole again.

Her voice shook. "I—I don't want to talk about Nicky."

"Nicky—" He repeated her son's name with such soft, paternal reverence she was taken aback.

Her pulse throbbed. "I-I said I won't talk—"

The corners of Joey's mouth curved coldly. "Why doesn't that surprise me? Well, you're going to talk about him. You're going to tell me everything. And the sooner, the better."

She swallowed, forgetting her nakedness beneath the blanket, forgetting she was his prisoner in this deserted cabin, forgetting everything except her fear for Nicky and what a disreputable movie star's sudden interest in the boy might do.

"Nobody's supposed to know about him."

"Not even me?"

"You?" Her voice was constricted. "Who do you think you are? You kidnapped me. Took advantage of me…"

"What?"

"You...you've been out of my life for years. Why did you drag me here against my will...to this isolated cabin?"

"I've been trying to find out about Nicky for a week. Last night was an accident—"

"How could you sink so low as to seduce me?"

His black gaze seared the soft cotton sheet and wool blanket molding her breasts and then the sleek flatness of her stomach. "You have it all backward, especially that last part, babe. It was the other way around. *You* seduced me. For your information, I put up one helluva fight...defending my...er...virtue."

"I don't believe you for one second. You're a monster."

"Maybe. But I'm your future husband, too."

Her eyes thinned to black-lashed, purple slits. "No."

"You have no other option, sweetheart. Unfortunately, neither do I."

She skittered toward the edge of the bed. "I'm marrying Larry. And I'm leaving now."

"I don't think so."

"You can't keep me here against my will."

"I don't intend to. When I'm through, you'll beg me to marry you."

"You're insane." Bunching her sheet above her breasts, her bare feet hit the cool wooden floor. She sprang out of his bed. "I'm going—"

When she took a step around the end of the bed, he cast an indifferent look out the dirty windows. "I wouldn't go out there, if I were you. Not unless you want to embarrass yourself."

She heaved herself past him toward the door that led to the porch. When he didn't stop her, she raced across the small room. She flung the door open just as her mother's baby-blue Cadillac swerved to a stop in front of the cabin.

Whorls of dust rose up around the shiny blue car. Joey's bland voice stung her like a whip. "Your family always was an in-your-face, nosy bunch. But maybe that's what being in politics does to folks. Hadn't you better put something on before we tell them our happy news? Or do you intend to discuss last night and our wedding plans wearing nothing but that sheet? Not that it isn't most...attractive. I sort of like the way it emphasizes your all-over blush.''

Her skin did feel on fire, but not just her skin. Inside, her arteries felt like they raced with molten lava. Never had she been so ashamed, so furious, so mortified.

''Heather dear—'' her mother called.

''Oh, no!''

Her parents were in the front seat of the car; someone else was in the back. For a long, hushed second Heather's mind made the Cadillac into a space ship and the familiar threesome into strange aliens frozen in some horrible, suspended form of animation. The three space creatures studied the girl in the sheet with an almost detached curiosity.

Then everybody recognized everybody.

Her father howled. Her mother screamed something about blood pressure.

Heather sank against the door.

She was living in a nightmare.

With a thin smile Heather notched her chin up. Then as if the sheet were her battle flag, she hoisted it higher to hide more bosom.

''Mother—'' she squeaked. ''Daddy—''

Her father's face was as dangerously black as an overripe plum.

She gasped when the sun made a golden halo of Larry's smooth hair as he gingerly eased himself out of the backseat.

''Why is Larry hobbling like a crippled old man?''

For no reason she imagined a huge reptilian tail thrashing back and forth on a wooden floor.

With his misshapen, blood-filled, black eye, Larry looked even more gruesome than her father.

Heather whirled on Joey. ''What did you do to him?''

"You should thank me."

"How could you—do this to him? To me?"

"It takes two to tango, babe," Joey purred. "You said you didn't want to know about last night." His black eyes laughed mirthlessly. "Hitch that damn sheet up, darling. It's slipping again. Those feminine treasures belong to me...and me alone now."

"You don't own me."

His broad grin disputed her claim.

"I'm going to marry Larry."

He shook his head. "Not in this lifetime."

Her face reddened. Her heart pounded.

"You!" She spat the word. "I was right to want you out of my life! You are trash. Just like Daddy says. You want to degrade me. You want to ruin him."

Joey's mouth thinned. "I want Nicky. Which means I'm stuck with you. I don't like it any better than you do."

When she sprang at him, her fingernails outstretched, Joey caught her easily. Her sheet tumbled to the floor, pooling at her ankles. Not that she cared as she thrashed naked in his arms. But he did, and he kicked the door shut to shield her from the others.

"Too bad we've got guests," he murmured. "This could be fun."

The low, controlled rumble of that hateful voice against her ear just made her burn hotter.

"I told you you'd lose your sheet, babe. Don't you even care—"

Outside the door, she heard the buzz of voices. Her parents and Laurence were mounting the stairs of the porch.

They didn't matter. Rage possessed her. Nothing, nothing mattered but wiping that infuriatingly smug smile off Joey's handsome face.

"I do hate you," she cried, her voice thick and taut as she fought him. "I do."

He grinned darkly. "I'll tell you exactly how I feel about

you…but later. When we're alone. After we're married and I've made love to you ten dozen more times.''

If she was hot, he was a blast furnace. Waves of body-heat burned through black denim to her skin.

''You aren't going to live that long,'' she cried.

''You wanna bet—''

Then his hands were all over her.

She fought him madly, trying to kick his shins, to pummel his thick, powerful chest. All too soon she realized that wriggling female flesh and her passionate anger were having an effect upon him that was entirely opposite to the one she desired.

Her black fury dissolved into alarm as a dangerous denim bulge swelled and hardened against her.

''There. There,'' he whispered when she was breathless and near fainting with rage. ''It's no use to fight me. I'll have you. You'll marry me— We'll make a fine couple— the big bad movie star and the senator's…er…*virtuous*…daughter. Especially if you still have your yen for mischief.''

With an iron grip he yanked her closer. When he thrust her against the wall, he began to shake.

''Damn you, Heather.'' He backed her against the rough, unpainted boards. ''You and your hypocritical parents made me feel like dirt.'' He paused. ''I want to feel nothing for you. Nothing. Do you understand? You destroyed me because of your damned daddy's political agenda. I didn't kill your brother. You weren't fair to blame me. If it's any comfort to you, I'm even unhappier about this mess than you are. When you seduced me last night, you trapped me in the same hell you are.''

It took a long time for her to meet his gaze. Near tears, she gulped in air. He closed his eyes. Then he fused his mouth to hers and pushed his tongue inside, ravaging her.

The heat of his kiss was hotter than anything she'd ever known. One taste of him, and fire burst like a blossom inside her. He flattened her soft breasts to his rock-solid chest. He cupped her buttocks.

Shameful longing dissolved her fury. In the next moment her lips parted of their own volition, and he ground himself against her.

"Oh, Joey... Joey...." She murmured in soft, breathy tones, arching toward him.

She felt his sudden, harsh, indrawn gasp.

When her fingers circled his neck, combing the long black hair at his nape, his angry kisses gentled. With a desperate hunger, he lifted her closer, and she melted against him.

"You ever done it against a wall, babe?"

"Don't ruin it," she whispered.

"You know we did." He laughed, remembering, too well.

She wanted him too much to care what he said. On a sigh of utter longing, she fashioned his name again.

"Joey."

"You see, darling. You're just as big a fool as I am."

She tried to jerk free of him, her face hot with shame, her heart slamming hard and quick. But he caught her hands and held her fast, interlacing his fingers with hers.

"After what you did to me last night, I can't let you marry that bastard. He's not adopting my kid either."

"Joey, Nicky's not yours."

"Last night you told me you've never slept with anybody else. So, don't lie about Nicky now." He pressed his mouth to the curve of her slender shoulder, his possessive lips both hot and tender. "No kid of mine is gonna grow up without a daddy. The sooner you get used to that fact, the better."

He shut his eyes. "You dated all those other guys. You had all those crazy relationships."

"How come you know so much?"

"You know how small towns are. Cass couldn't wait to

tell me." He paused. "I'm not letting you go. Not after last night." He kissed her, again and again. Each time his mouth touched hers, her blood surged. Instinctively she molded herself to him. His mouth was a brand searing her lips, her throat, her eyelids.

"You are mine, senator's daughter."

When he finally stopped kissing her, she slumped against the wall. With purposeful strides he crossed the room. Yanking a dresser drawer open, he pulled out a loosely woven cotton shirt, a rope, and a pair of faded jeans. These he pitched at her before he shoved the door open and stomped across the threshold to greet her family.

As she shakily dressed and smoothed her hair, her senses slowly came back to her. Her father and her mother and her fiancé were outside waiting for some sort of rational explanation.

There wasn't one.

As the mischievous daughter sandwiched in between a brilliant, studious sister and a coveted only son, Heather's parents hadn't appreciated her penchant for devilment. Nor had they liked her soft heart. No matter how fiercely they'd disciplined her or how hard she'd tried to be good, her virtue never lasted. Her soft heart had made her easy pickings for quite a few unsuitable boyfriends who'd cried on her shoulder. Still, for as long as she could remember she'd wanted them to be as proud of her as they'd been of her brother and sister.

Last night, Joey had destroyed all chance of that.

She'd slept with him. He knew about Nicky. He was forcing her to marry him.

Joey Fasano had always brought out the worst in her. He always would.

For the first time in her life she hated him for it.

Six

"**M**y daughter? Married? To you?" Her father jabbed a finger menacingly toward the screen door. "Heather! Get out here!"

Heather pressed her splayed hand against the screen door, cringing when the hinge groaned.

At the sight of her daughter's wild, frizzed hair and the sheets tumbling off Joey's disheveled bed, Nellie stared, her concerned, maternal squint freezing on Heather's swollen lips and the masculine shirt falling softly over her daughter's unrestrained breasts.

"What happened to your pretty yellow dress, Heather Ann?"

"Somebody ripped it off her," Joey said coldly.

"What!" Her parents glared at Joey as if he were a monster.

"Don't look at me," he said with an outraged air of innocence that didn't quite suit him.

Heather tried to smile. Why couldn't she simply tell them

she wasn't Joey's girl, and she wasn't about to marry him? She needed to tell Joey the whole truth, too.

Instead, she stumbled across the rough planks as mute with shame as a guilty child. When the screen banged noisily behind her, Joey shoved a chair toward her father.

Travis glared at her, his silence so thick and hostile, the soft cotton collar of Joey's shirt tightened around her neck, cutting off her breath. As always, ever since she'd been a little girl, her father's disapproval overwhelmed her.

Maybe if she hadn't been wearing Joey's clothes, she wouldn't have felt at such a total loss. But the unmade bed and Joey's cotton shirt and baggy jeans roped at her waist branded her as his. His fresh male scent clung to his clothes and was a constant reminder of the intimacies they'd shared.

Her father's hard eyes probed her flushed face. "Your dress was torn off you. And Fasano's boy here says he's gonna marry you, Heather Ann."

When Heather only chewed her bottom lip, Travis whirled on Joey. "Tell me you're lying."

Leaning negligently against the railing, Joey gave them all a wolfish grin. "After last night, marriage is the only honorable option."

"When hell freezes over," Travis yelled.

Heather buried her hot face in her hands.

Joey's grin deepened her blush. "The devil had better dig out his long underwear."

"Your sordid sex life with Hollywood tramps is legendary!" Travis roared even louder. "Why would somebody like you want to marry a girl like Heather anyway?"

Heather winced. She fisted her hands. Just as quickly she opened her fingers and flexed them.

"There's no accounting for personal taste, now is there?" Joey said. "Maybe I'm just a sentimental guy."

"Heather—" Her father leaned toward her. "What do you have to say? Look at me, girl. You know I've got a tough race. The opposition will have a field day with this. Is this more of your childish rebellion—?''

Quick, mutinous tears burned her lashes. Looking away, she swiped at her eyes. Always, always her father cared about himself instead of her. When she'd gotten pregnant, all he'd thought of was his career. When she'd told him about Nicky, again he'd worried about himself.

Always he thought the worst of her. Why try to defend herself? Alison had been the smart, disciplined daughter he loved. When she'd gotten sick, he'd stayed at the hospital day and night by her side. Heather should know she couldn't ever please him.

While he studied her, Heather focused on the green wall of cypress trees fringing the creek. The sun blazed mercilessly through their leaves, shooting brilliant prisms onto the water. Despite the heat, the bluebonnets were glorious blue patches in the green pastures.

''*Heather Ann*— Answer me.''

Why? You never listen. She tightened her mouth and glued her gaze on the shining trees.

Travis turned on Joey. ''She must be dull pickings after your usual tramps—''

''Maybe the tramps…gave me an appetite for a lady.''

Jealousy knifed her, and she moaned.

Dark eyes glittering, Joey uncoiled his long body from the railing and strolled to her side. His heavy arm slid around her. ''All joking aside. Your daughter is the woman I want—''

Forgetting she hated him, Heather nestled into him. Only after her father's glare, did she remember she should push him away. Joey's arm tensed, holding her there.

She was living in a nightmare. No, this was hell, and Joey was the devil. Had he hopped out of bed yesterday morning with the goal to ruin her life?

''If you do this dreadful thing, dear, what will everybody

say?'' her mother whispered. ''Do you want your father to lose?''

''You're out of your mind to marry him,'' Laurence chimed.

''Shut up,'' Joey said. ''All of you.''

''Why won't any of you listen to me?'' Heather pushed at Joey. ''I am not marrying him. I hate you,'' she whispered, looking up at him.

Joey's arms tightened; his gaze smoldered when he smiled. ''Ditto, babe.''

''I've hated you for six years.''

''Ditto.''

''Don't say that!''

Joey's smile broadened. ''See, we're already arguing like an old married couple. We have problems. We'll have to work them out.''

Travis slapped his hands on his knees and jumped up. ''This craziness has gone far enough. It's hot. I'm tired of wasting valuable time.''

''So am I.'' Joey's voice was equally hard. ''Let's cut to the chase. Heather was my girl. I got her pregnant. I wasn't good enough, and you wanted to look like the perfect father to your constituents. So, you told her to say our baby died. Well, I found out about Nicky.''

''What?'' Travis looked thunderstruck.

''I know she's been living in Louisiana, so people wouldn't put two and two together. Larry here is going to marry her, dream up some story about my kid and then conveniently adopt him when your constituents are distracted by other matters.''

Silently, Heather wrapped her arms around her body and squeezed herself as her father slumped into his chair like a balloon going down with a sudden puncture. Joey was ruining her chance to please her parents and to give Nicky anything approaching a normal childhood. She didn't know what to do or say. She'd never been able to think clearly in a crisis, especially when Joey was around to mix her up.

The steady hum of the cicadas in the distance only made the heavy silence on that shady porch seem thicker.

"You people lied," Joey said. "But the only lie I care about is Heather's. She put me in hell. She owes me—big time. And she's gonna pay."

Heather felt a cold, hollow knot of fear in her stomach. Marriage—to an infamous movie star whose scandalous career would damage her father's. Once things had seemed so simple. Once she'd thought marriage to Joey would mean love, compromise, commitment, tenderness, a vine-covered cottage. She had wanted his children, imagined shared laughter and long sensual nights. Never had she thought of marriage as a prison sentence, shackling her to a stranger who despised her.

Maybe she should tell them all the whole truth.

· Her mind spun backward.

She'd had no choice.

Oh, Daddy. Oh, Mom.

All she'd ever wanted was to please them. She wanted to fling herself into her parents' arms, to explain the whole crazy series of events that had led to this, to beg their forgiveness for always, always getting into trouble and hurting them. But they'd never really understood her any more than she'd understood them. They thought their rules were the only rules. You didn't love cute boys that were fun. You married into a certain class, behaved a certain way, lived according to their standards. You thought other people's thoughts. You surrendered your own life to public service. You kept fatherless babies a secret. She had loved Nicky too much to abandon him. She'd been afraid to tell them the truth; she was still afraid.

But Joey was no safe harbor. What would happen to her? To Nicky? Would marriage to Joey mean her family would be forced to distance themselves from her? Could Nicky have a normal life? And what kind of man was Joey now? She rarely read anything good about him.

Remotely, as if she were very far away, she heard the harsh drone of Joey's voice.

"Either she marries me, or I go to the tabloids. I'll tell them I slept with Senator Wade's wild daughter six years ago."

"You're trash," Travis said. "Just like your father was."

"I'll give them pictures. You'd be surprised at the pictures your daughter took of me. They were so racy, I had to develop them myself."

"You wouldn't."

"Publicity, any kind, is good for a man in my business," Joey said. "Scandal sells movie tickets. Too bad it doesn't work that way with elections."

"You sorry son-of— I saw you for what you were early on. This is nothing but an act of cheap revenge."

"I'll say Nicky's mine," Joey continued.

At the opposite end of the porch, Laurence sprang to his feet.

"Sit! Or I tell them what you pulled in the boathouse. They'll love me after they hear that."

Larry's misshapen eye twitched. "Liar!"

"His no-good brother drugged her. Then he attacked—"

"Drugged—" Nellie moaned. For the first time her shocked gaze contained concern for her daughter.

"You disgust me." Laurence's voice was self-righteous, but he was visibly shaking now.

"Ditto." Under Joey's glare, Laurence backed down. "You've got an hour before I make that call. If you have your wedding as planned tonight, you'll have more paparazzi than wedding guests."

"I don't need an hour," Heather said. "Go ahead. Call them. I—I can't marry you. I—I can't live without closeness...without...." She'd been about to say love.

Joey's hard eyes locked with hers, eviscerating that tender word into a lump of ash in her throat.

"I'll take Nicky away," she rushed on, desperate. "To Europe. Maybe Italy. I'll never come back. You won't have to worry about me hurting your precious election."

Travis's face blackened. "Oh, no you won't. The press would eat me alive. You'll do the smart thing for once and marry him."

At her father's harsh voice, her head jerked toward him. "What?"

"It's the only way," Travis said. "If you leave, and he talks, everyone would believe him. I'm ruined. I'll never live it down."

Joey's eyes glittered as he watched the confusion of turbulent emotions erupt across Heather's face—willfulness, hopelessness, despair.

When the blaze dimmed, she stilled. "That's what you really want, Daddy? Mother?"

When they nodded, Heather turned to Joey. Finding nothing in his hard, impassive features and cold smile to give her hope, she managed a dull whisper. "You don't know what you're doing. Nicky's my son. Not yours."

"We're getting married," Joey said, but his face was grim, as if a deep pain tore him, too. "Leave," he ordered her parents and Laurence. "I want to talk to my future wife." He fairly snarled that last word.

Heather was shaking by the time the three of them filed off the porch. Nobody looked back or told her goodbye. Feeling lost and abandoned, Heather heard their car doors slam. The Cadillac's tires pinged loose gravel against the house before racing away and vanishing in the trees.

Joey's black eyes nailed her.

"What? What do you have to scowl about?" she whispered.

"You."

Here's a **HOT** offer for you!

Get set for a sizzling summer read...

with **2 FREE ROMANCE BOOKS**
and a **FREE MYSTERY GIFT!**
NO CATCH! NO OBLIGATION TO BUY!

Simply complete and return this card and you'll get **FREE BOOKS, A FREE GIFT** and much more!

- The first shipment is yours to keep, **absolutely free!**
- Enjoy the convenience of romance books, delivered right to your door, before they're available in the stores!
- Take advantage of special low pricing for **Reader Service Members only!**
- After receiving your free books we hope you'll want to remain a subscriber. But the choice is always yours—to continue or cancel anytime at all! So why not take us up on this fabulous invitation with no risk of any kind. You'll be glad you did!

326 SDL CPSR

225 SDL CPSJ
S-D-05/99

Name:	
	(Please Print)
Address:	Apt.#:
City:	
State/Prov.:	Zip/ Postal Code:

▼ DETACH HERE AND MAIL CARD TODAY! ▼

The Silhouette Reader Service™ —Here's How it Works:

Accepting your 2 free books and mystery gift places you under no obligation to buy anything. You may keep the books and gift and return the shipping statement marked "cancel." If you do not cancel, about a month later we'll send you 6 additional novels and bill you just $3.12 each in the U.S., or $3.49 each in Canada, plus 25¢ delivery per book and applicable taxes if any.* That's the complete price and — compared to the cover price of $3.75 in the U.S. and $4.25 in Canada — it's quite a bargain! You may cancel at any time, but if you choose to continue, every month we'll send you 6 more books, which you may either purchase at the discount price or return to us and cancel your subscription.

*Terms and prices subject to change without notice. Sales tax applicable in N.Y. Canadian residents will be charged applicable provincial taxes and GST.

If offer card is missing write to: Silhouette Reader Service, 3010 Walden Ave., P.O. Box 1867, Buffalo, NY 14240-1867

BUSINESS REPLY MAIL
FIRST-CLASS MAIL   PERMIT NO. 717   BUFFALO, NY

POSTAGE WILL BE PAID BY ADDRESSEE

SILHOUETTE READER SERVICE
3010 WALDEN AVE
PO BOX 1867
BUFFALO NY 14240-9952

NO POSTAGE
NECESSARY
IF MAILED
IN THE
UNITED STATES

"You got what you wanted. Didn't you? Well, didn't you?"

"Not quite."

She began to shake. "Why are you doing this, if you don't want marriage any more than I do?"

"I told you—Nicky," he ground out.

Nicky. Of course, he thought Nicky was his. Again, she thought about telling him the truth.

Later. She could cross that bridge later if she had to. So, instead she said, "What about us? What sort of happiness can two people who hate each other possibly find together?"

His predatory black gaze slid furiously from her eyes to her lips, passing from her breasts down her hips, before slowly, possessively returning to her face. His sarcastic drawl heated with deliberate, sexual menace. "After last night, one kind of pleasure does come to mind."

Every nerve in her body trilled with unwanted awareness of him. She kept her gaze carefully averted, but guilt burned her, guilt about Nicky, guilt about the sexual intimacies they'd shared, guilt about the way just looking at him made her feel.

"I can't forget how hot and takable you felt against that wall a while ago, Heather. We could finish that—"

"Would you quit? I *won't* sleep with you again. That's not part of this sordid bargain."

"Says who?"

"Me."

His eyes narrowed. "As if you have the whole say. Your father, *the senator,* ordered you to marry me. Daddy's little girl agreed. Just like you probably agreed to marry Larry. You've never lived your own life or made your own decisions. You never will. So, I'll run you the same way he has."

She put her hands on her hips. "No!"

Relentlessly he held her gaze. "We're getting married! We're going to sleep together!"

"No."

When she tried to scoot away from him, he levered himself toward her. As she bolted, he spread muscled arms wide, blocking her escape.

"You are mine," he said. "Completely mine."

Faltering, she fell back. He followed her like a cat stalking a mouse. Her spine hit the front door, the doorknob ramming into her back. She cried out. He closed in, putting a heavy arm on either side of her slim shoulders. Leaning into her, he caged her.

She didn't want him so close. His massive chest hovering mere inches above her face shook and unnerved her. Her gaze climbed his tall muscular body, up his broad shoulders until she met his intense gaze. Never had he seemed more ruthlessly determined or more dangerous.

In that charged instant, she remembered how he'd branded her with his kisses. A tint of fiery color crept into her cheeks when she realized he was savoring the same memory.

"See what I mean?" His curt voice grew huskier, silkier. "We both know this isn't smart, but we can't help ourselves."

The sun came out again. Its brilliance shone behind him, casting his features into darkness, so that she could no longer read his eyes. But the sexual threat of his huge body and the purposeful stillness of his wide-legged stance was unmistakable.

Suddenly she was afraid of him again.

But for all the wrong reasons.

She drew in a quick breath and forgot to release it. To her he had always been and always would be—irresistible.

How easily he'd once talked her into stuffing Reverend Scott's wife's panties into her own plastic doll's trunk and then tying that parcel of mischief to the tail of her daddy's most temperamental stallion.

Joey's low voice deepened to raspy velvet. "You want me, babe. I know it. You know it." He lifted her hand to his lips, cupped it, and blew a warm kiss into her palm. "You were the one who slipped this hand inside my jeans and grabbed me."

She yanked her offending fingers away and hid them behind her back. Her throat went tight, her mouth dry. "I didn't—" She nearly choked. "I wouldn't! You're... you're just saying that to scare me."

"You wouldn't let go, babe. You took me inside your pretty lips and made me a very happy man."

"Somebody ought to wash your mouth out."

"Why don't you start...with your tongue!" he taunted. "Shut up!"

"You're just mad 'cause you want to. Lucky for you...I don't hold your wanton appetites against you."

Lucky.... "You said I was drug—"

"Well, you aren't drugged now. You still want me."

"Why, you conceited...pathetic liar. I—I don't."

She hated the way his grin spread across his face and made him so devastatingly handsome.

"I'll grant you the conceited part. But I'm no liar. A while ago, when I kissed you against that wall, it was all I could do to peel your legs and arms off me."

All her life she had wanted to be good and proper. The trouble was she wanted Joey Fasano more.

"You'll have to use force to make me sleep with you."

"I don't think so." His voice was silken, his smile slow and easy.

Oh, how she hated the way his soft, determined words could lure her.

"Remember how it was in my hideout when you were a naughty little girl. I wanted to see. You wanted to show.

Why don't you show me something now. If I like what I see, maybe I'll return the favor.''

"Grow up, Joey."

"I *am* full grown."

He grinned when she blushed. Still, her nipples peaked at his invitation. Her fingertips itched to strip herself and then him. It was all she could do to keep her hands off the buttons of her cotton shirt. She wanted to undo them, one by one, slowly, and watch his black eyes start to glow like living coals until he couldn't stand it and stripped her shirt off her himself. Until he ripped her jeans apart and unfastened his, until he took her against that white, unpainted wall in broad daylight.

If he'd been born bad, so had she.

His sexy burst of laughter turned her face scarlet.

She shivered. "You're an oversexed fiend."

"Takes one to know one." The familiar taunt brought back his childhood habit of slinging that particular insult at her when no fresh material sprang to mind.

"I'm not a child...."

"It's about time you figured that out. You've been so busy trying to please other people, you couldn't accept yourself. You're hot in the sack and pretty as a peach. We're getting married, and there's no reason not to indulge ourselves in the one pleasure we can salvage from this disaster. You're dying to strip for me, to show me what you've got—so go ahead! You want me."

Guilt and fury that she was so transparent washed over her. For an instant she glared at him. Maybe she was furious, but for six years she hadn't once felt this alive.

She wanted to marry him, and she wanted to sleep with him.

Oh, no, no. She couldn't, *wouldn't,* admit that.

Defiantly she rammed her fists against his wide chest, relishing a fierce joy when she caught him off guard. He fell backward, and she lit out for the trees.

Behind her, she heard his rich laughter. "I just put your own thoughts into words! In another minute you would've peeled every stitch off."

"Would not! You're lewd, crude—"

"Would too!"

At the crack of a twig under his boot, a blackberry bush stirred near the dam. Seeking the glitter of golden hair among those sparkling leaves, Joey strode even faster toward the dam.

An emerald canopy, aglow with sunshine, roofed the creek. Pinpoints of reflected sunlight glimmered like diamonds on the clear green wavelets splashing over the rocky dam. So anxious was he to find Heather, he cursed the spongy earth that made him sink squishily into the tall lush grasses that grew along the sloping banks. That lazy Cass needed to get down here with a mower.

She had run from him. He should let her be for a while and not let her know he cared so much. Why couldn't he?

"Heather—" Joey yelled.

Above him, a bright voice chirped. "Up here, Hollywood."

He frowned when she sprang out of a cypress tree, holding onto a fraying rope Cass should have changed last summer. Joey's heart skipped a beat as her slim body sailed across limestone rocks, across the glittering creek and then back at him. She let go, and her shapely form plunked into the squishy wet grass, splashing mud onto his boots.

"Sorry," she teased.

"If that rope had broken—" he began, furious.

Her eyes blazed. "It didn't." She pursed her cherry-bright red mouth.

An angry pulse began to beat in his temple. "You should be more careful. You shouldn't play…such dangerous games."

"Why do you care?"

He clenched his teeth. The sunlight shone in her hair. She looked way too cute in his huge shirt. She had too much power over him.

"How come you wouldn't marry me yourself?" he demanded, stunned by his own question.

"What?"

"You're marrying me because your father ordered you—"

"Oh, that—" She waved offhandedly. "Surely...you didn't expect me to...to want to marry you myself."

"Heaven forbid." He swore under his breath.

"Then how come you're so grouchy? You got what you wanted." Her pert face stared up at him. "So, everything's settled, right?"

"Right."

Her gaze fastened on his. Then she laughed, emboldened suddenly, surer. The new glint of confidence in her gaze made him feel anything but settled.

A leaf falling through the air snagged on a loose, golden curl. He reached toward it, and then stopped, afraid to touch even a wisp of her yellow hair or that dry leaf because if he she felt as warm and boneless as she had on the porch, his desire might become unquenchable.

But the dangling leaf begged to be smoothed away from her forehead. Her lips glistened, tempting his.

Her silence grew tremulous.

Against his better judgment, he cupped her chin and brought her lips closer. She gasped. Above them leaves murmured. Birds sang. Cicadas thrummed.

Not that he noticed. Her warm breath seared him, her body trembled every time he touched her. Her heat seeped slowly into him.

They weren't plastered together, but her nearness made him melt.

He closed his eyes. It felt dangerously good to want her. It felt like coming home. Almost he could forget she'd told him their baby was dead and thrown him out. Almost he could forget her family thought he was dirt. Almost he could believe it could be like it was when they were kids and madly in love.

Caution seized him.

He forced his lashes apart. Without a word, he let her go.

"Why did you stop?" she whispered.

"You've got a leaf," he muttered. "Up there—"

"Why don't you take it out for me?"

He swallowed.

"What are you afraid of?"

"Nothing, damn it."

With a quirky smile, she reached up and smoothed the leaf from her curls.

As it fluttered through her fingers, her mouth fashioned his name.

His breathing roughened. For a second he thought if he didn't touch her and make love to her in those tall wet grasses, he'd fly to pieces.

Instead, he ground his bootheel into the soft earth and pivoted.

Her quick girlish giggle sent him stomping off toward his cabin.

With the sunshine glowing through the stained glass windows of the charming, limestone church and the organ music resounding beneath the rafters of the vaulted ceiling, there was no sign that the impending ceremony was not wished for by all.

A last-minute change of grooms?

Reverend Scott, whose principles were rigid and unyielding, had been mystified at first, then appalled to learn that the notorious Joey Fasano who'd once made his wife the laughingstock of the whole town really was going to take Laurence's place beside Heather.

"Such a thing is unheard of. Miss Wade, I cannot sanction such an impulsive, self-destructive act."

"You could *if* you wanted to." Joey had held out a large check. "Heather tells me your congregation is having difficulty raising money to remodel the sanctuary. Could I make a small donation toward your worthy cause?"

When the pastor did not take his check, Joey laid it on his desk so that everyone could reflect on the lengthy string of zeroes. "I assure you there will be an equally large donation from the senator who wants this marriage as much as I do."

Senator Wade almost choked.

"Let me know what you decide," Joey said.

If Reverend Scott's downward glance was swift, his decision after the senator nodded was even speedier.

"As you wish," Scott said coldly.

Joey placed a hand on the check, forcing the reverend to stay.

"Maybe now's not the right time. But did I ever apologize for stealing Mrs. Scott's undies off your clothesline?"

An angry flush bloomed above the reverend's tight white collar. "It's way too late for an apology, young man."

"Still, I do apologize," Joey said in a low, contrite tone.

Trapped in a small Sunday-school room near the chapel with a cop at the door, Joey and Mac hurriedly dressed. Joey's black tie dangled untied around his neck as he inserted black enamel studs into his cuffs. Through the thin walls, he could hear the buzz of gossip in the chapel. The political blue-bloods probably blamed him for the frenzied clamor of the paparazzi outside.

Damn.

Even though the only person Joey had invited was Mac, the church was packed. Circling helicopters and throngs of newsmen had turned the wedding into a media circus.

Travis was as outraged as Reverend Scott. Heather had turned white when a journalist phoned to ask if she was pregnant. Joey had grabbed the phone and slammed it down. Then he'd called Mac.

Like so many events in Joey's life, his wedding had become a public ordeal to get through.

"Man. Your Heather's really classy." Mac pulled Joey's pressed jacket off its valet's hanger and shook it out. When Joey said nothing, Mack slid the jacket over Joey's straining muscles. "Either the jacket's a little tight, or you're a little uptight—"

Joey flexed his arms. "It'll do."

"I like your Heather," Mac said. "She's a real lady."

"She tries."

Mac's intrusive presence, the organ music, the dramatic murmurs from the pews, and the wail of sirens outside made the prospect of marriage suddenly too real for Joey.

"I can't believe you're doing this," Mac persisted.

Anger pooled in Joey's black gaze. "Neither can I."

"You thank a girl I never heard of for your Oscar. You leave my party. You don't call us for a week. Then—bam! You want me bring your tux, arrange a wedding license, fly some kid from Louisiana here, tell Daniella she can keep the diamonds you rented Oscar night as a goodbye present. You tell me to get out here and be your best man. What do you think I am—a genie with a towel wrapped around my head?"

"It's complicated."

"Is she pregnant—"

"Not you, too...."

"But the kid from Louisiana's involved—"

Joey shot Mac a guilty glance.

"So, he's yours?"

"She won't say. But she's been hiding him in Louisiana for five years. A bastard grandson wouldn't look too good for the senator."

"Gotcha. Look. Marriage isn't an easy proposition under circumstances like these...especially in our business. But it's bound to fail if you have a bad attitude."

Sirens screamed outside in the parking lot. Joey frowned. "Can the lecture."

"I never told you this before. I had to marry Titania."

"Not now, Mac—"

"You're gonna hear what I'm saying, brother."

Joey flipped one of the venetian blinds open. The parking lot was jammed with cars, police vehicles, reporters. Those morons with their microphones and long lenses loved turning his life into a living hell.

"You think we've always had this perfect marriage," Mac persisted. "Well, we didn't. I blamed her for trapping me. You know how girls like me, how I never so much as touch one—"

Curious, Joey released the venetian blind, pivoting as it popped back in place. He stared at Mac hard.

"Hey, I used to chase tail. Titania caught me. Man, I nearly messed everything up but good. She kicked me out. I found out quick how much I loved her. I wanted her back. I wanted my life back. She wanted a divorce."

"So—"

"When she took me back, I didn't get a night's sleep for a year. Any time my head hit the pillow, bam, she'd start to cry about those other girls. She'd want to know if I loved her. I'd have to hold her and say how sorry I was. Over and over and over, till I was rum-dumb with exhaustion. Titania's one woman you don't mess with. After a year, she finally said, 'You stay with me, means you stay with me. Period. No more girls.' Brother, she taught me women run the show."

"I let Heather run me once. She's what made my life go so crazy."

Mac would have offered more unwanted advice had not

Reverend Scott cracked the door and grimly signaled it was time.

"Well, Mac?" Joey muttered. "You ready to take a stroll up that aisle? Or are you having too much fun playing marriage counselor?"

"Is it just my imagination, or does the saintly reverend detest you?"

"I don't think it's your imagination. His most memorable sermon was about me. Ranted on and on about me being the devil's spawn. I was pretty cocky for a while." Joey's grin held dark mischief. "You'd think he'd be grateful. If it weren't for the devil...and his...er...misbehaving spawn, the sanctimonious old windbag would be out of a job."

Seven

"**I** will never, ever forgive you—" Heather whispered brokenly. "Daddy will probably lose the election, and *he'll* never forgive *me*—"

Before she could strengthen her attack, Joey's Learjet hit turbulence. She was bounced so hard against the buckle of her clasped safety belt, she gripped his arm.

"Sorry," she whispered faintly, releasing him, resenting him even more for her fear and weakness.

He looked up from his magazine and shot her a tense grin. "Be my guest. Grab me anytime…anywhere…."

"Would you stop with the sexual innuendo?"

His eyes darkened to midnight black. "This is our wedding night."

"I told you I'm not in the mood," she snapped.

"What if I am?" He stroked a finger delicately beneath her chin, and she stiffened. But not before he saw the blush that betrayed the hot tingle burning through her.

"You couldn't possibly make me want—"

"Hey, don't tempt me to prove you wrong."

When he stared at her for another long moment, Heather shivered at the thought that he might gather her to him, close those long, sexy lashes, and kiss her.

"As tabloid stud-muffin king, I stake my...er...lurid reputation on the fact that I can make you want me." He backhanded his fingers through his hair. "So, beware, babe."

Then he shut his eyes as if he meant to kiss her. Shutting hers, too, pursing her lips, she leaned toward him. When nothing happened, she opened her eyes to his broad, know-it-all grin.

"See there!"

"Would you stop it?"

"Just proving my point. You were all puckered up. You wanted me to kiss you."

"Did not!"

"But this is all you get...for now." He blew her a sexy kiss and laughed.

At her scowl, he lowered his black head over his magazine.

She gritted her teeth. "As I was saying, I will *never* forgive—"

"Caught the first broadcast." Joey punched the button that made his seat bolt to an upright position. "How about a glass of wine?"

"Absolutely not!"

"Why don't you read something? Look out the window? Relax?"

"Impossible with you here."

"Do you remember the time I seduced you with a box of chocolates?"

"Oh!"

"Okay. I'll be good." He levered his broad shoulder away from her and resumed reading.

She persisted. "Our wedding had to be the most embarrassing moment of my entire life."

Silence. Then he flipped a page noisily. She saw a color spread of him on horseback.

The musky fragrance of his cologne wafted toward her, sharpening her awareness of how good he smelled, of just how physically attractive he was even now when he was pretending to ignore her.

Heather sniffed. "After putting me through that ordeal in the church, after putting my mother and my father…and Julia through it, how can you be so vulgar as to insist on this…this farce of a honeymoon…in Vegas—"

He grinned. "Easy."

He turned another page of his magazine. More glossy pictures of him on horseback lay across his lap. Under the shadowy brim of a cowboy hat, he had several days' worth of dark stubble. He looked wild and bad and dangerous as he lassoed a running woman with long black braids in the desert.

"You made our wedding a public joke. Why did you have to drag Nicky there? You knew my father didn't want anybody to know about him. At least not before—"

A muscle twitched in his jaw. "Not till you were properly married—to Roth." His black gaze burned her. "Your father runs you, not me, understand? Maybe after nearly six damned years, I was anxious to see *my* son. Maybe I thought our marriage was too important not to include him."

"I'll never live it down."

"How was I supposed to know what he'd do? Hey, I'm sorry you feel bad. I might even be sorry your parents feel bad someday, but, hell, did it ever occur to you that maybe turnabout is fair play?"

Turnabout? "Did you bring him there just to get revenge?"

"No!" Joey exhaled an angry breath. "Oh, hell, I don't

know why I do what I do sometimes. Maybe I just don't want my son to be a secret everybody has to be ashamed of. I know what that's like. As a kid, I always felt awful around your family. For some reason your dad hated mine. And you were always so sure he'd dislike me, you kept our friendship a secret. I used to dream of you telling your family about me, of you demanding that they accept me. But you never did. You never wanted your parents, especially your father, to know about us. Later, when we were older, you snuck out to date me. I wasn't *ever* good enough.''

Heather stared past him and wondered why there was a silly lump in her throat. The lights on the ground seemed to be rushing toward her, but it was the other way around. The jet was speeding down toward earth, through clouds and night-dark and stars.

An impenetrable mask covered Joey's features as he glared at her.

''The whole damn town knew we loved each other, but you wouldn't tell your parents,'' he said quietly. ''I always felt like I was trash because you were too ashamed of me to admit to them you liked me.''

''I—I…wasn't ashamed. Not of you, anyway.''

''Then?''

''I—I was ashamed of the fun things we did together. I was afraid of my parents. Afraid they'd make me stop seeing you, and I couldn't do those things with you anymore.''

''Oh, really? Remember that night we were in Ben's car after that last dance?''

As if she could ever forget.

''How come you asked Ben to step on the gas when we saw that cop?''

''How can you ask me that?'' she whispered.

''Be honest. It was so your father wouldn't find out that you'd been with me.''

''You don't understand.''

"Oh, yeah, I do."

"You don't understand how it was with him."

"What exactly were you feeling that night, Heather?"

She didn't answer, and he drew a long breath. "If you're ever gonna grow up, you have to face what happened and how you felt."

Color reddened her cheeks.

"When Ben let the three of us out on that rutted road and raced away with that cop on his tail, you didn't feel proud of me. You were scared of your father and ashamed of me."

"No! No!"

"Yes! Later, when we heard those damned sirens and then when we found Ben in that tangled pile of metal, you didn't turn to me. He was *my* best friend! I loved him, too! You were pregnant with my baby, but you ran from me."

"They found out about us soon enough."

Scant inches separated their bodies. She felt him stiffen. There were old barriers as well as new between them.

"Not that night, they didn't." His harsh statement rocked her. "Ben was dead. You wouldn't even look at me. You ran off with Roth, so nobody would guess you'd been with me. You never spoke to me again alone either, not even during the funeral."

"They had enough to grieve about."

"And because I was low-class and poor. An inappropriate companion for the lovely Miss Wade. How do you think I felt? Did you care? I slept on the kitchen floor by our phone, but you never called. Not once. No. You didn't say a word till you told me our baby was dead and to get out of your life."

Heather felt tears pricking her eyes. "I'm sorry."

"Maybe sorry's not good enough, babe."

"What do you want from me?"

"Maybe the truth for a change." His voice softened. "Or a new beginning."

She closed her eyes and tilted her chin defiantly. "It isn't that easy. You're pushing me too fast."

"That's the way it is. Last night we slept with each other, and it was great," he said. "Your folks know. The whole damn world knows, including your precious daddy's voters. What's so damned terrible about us having sex? We're grown-ups now. I married you, didn't I?" A glint of possessive mockery flashed in his eyes. "I'm willing to claim Nicky, too. He's my son, and I don't care who knows it."

Violence stormed within her when she remembered his threat to go to the tabloids.

He's not yours. Any more than he's mine.

She couldn't tell him that though. Not yet. She understood his feelings better than he knew. She knew what it was to love a child she hadn't given birth to. There was no way she could question Joey's instant love for Nicky when she'd started loving him the minute he was born.

Julia had been so shattered after Ben's death, she'd been too numb to feel anything for her own baby. When he'd bellowed piteously in his crib, Julia had fled to the rose garden, and Heather had gone to his crib. Cuddling the tight-fisted, muscular bundle to her bosom, changing him, feeding him—smothering him with all the love she'd felt denied to her by her own parents, with all the love she would have given her own baby, Nicky had become hers. Then every day he'd reminded her more and more of Joey, her lost love. As Julia had sought spiritual answers, Heather's adopting Nicky had become Heather's most heartfelt desire. Maybe she hadn't worried enough about the consequences.

"I want to know and love Nicky," Joey repeated.

Heather's teeth began to chatter, and not from the cold.

"Oh, what's going to happen to the three of us?" she whispered, suddenly frantic.

"We're going to be a family."

A part of her longed for that.

Joey bent his head over his magazine again. His handsome features were half in shadow; the carved edges of his face that were visible revealed superb self-confidence. He thought this forced marriage solved everything. Never had his male point of view seemed more maddeningly simplistic.

Her life wouldn't be such a mess if he hadn't rushed her. If he'd given her more time, maybe she could have figured out what to do. Making decisions during a crisis was definitely not her strong suit. As a result, three lives were in limbo.

Suddenly, remembering the humiliation of their wedding, she wanted to wring his neck. But just imagining her fingers on his warm, dark skin made her feel hot and shivery.

Why, she was as disgustingly craven as a lovesick fan. So many women lusted after him she could never be special.

"We can't be a family." Her low, jealous voice pierced the thick silence. "Not the way you live!"

He slammed his magazine shut. "Just what do you mean?"

"Pick up a tabloid, stud-king."

His black eyebrows knitted. His sharp gaze zeroed in on her face. "I'll give you a movie-star-wife survival tip. Don't read tabloids."

"How else can I learn the truth—"

He glanced at her, saw her genuine pain, and his worried expression suddenly grew both poignantly tender and intense. "I'm not the one who's afraid of the truth." Lightly he brought a fingertip to her cheek. "Now am I?"

At his gentle touch, she expelled a ragged breath. His physical attraction was too compelling; there was no way she could trust him.

"What about...other women?"

"For the record," he rasped softly. "As long as we're married, there won't be any."

Mentally she fought to shake away her pleasure at what sounded like a heartfelt promise. "How can I believe—"

His eyebrow lifted. "I was teasing about the stud-king bit." A telling blush stole across his dark face. "Hey, I'm not as hot as you think…with other women. So, there won't be any." Joey smiled. "So, believe."

His words and that beguiling smile and unaccountable blush caused an insane weakness in her knees and a strange tightening in the pit of her stomach. Why couldn't she brush off his promise as carelessly as he'd probably uttered it? And why couldn't she erase as well the way her skin burned where his finger had caressed her?

But there was Nicky. Joey thought he was the boy's father, and he wanted to be a good father. He'd been so natural with Nicky when he'd told the boy goodbye on her mother's front porch, too.

Nicky had burst into tears when Heather had said he couldn't go on their honeymoon. Even though they were late, Joey had knelt down and explained what a honeymoon was. Even when Nicky had flung himself into Joey's arms and demanded postcards and books filled with fun-facts about Vegas, Joey had remained both firm and patient.

After promising to deliver those goods, Joey had picked the little boy up and carried him to the limousine to give him a final hug goodbye.

Nicky's eyes had danced with fresh excitement as he'd fingered the shiny chrome on Joey's limo. "Can I have another present? A real present?"

"Like what?"

"A water gun?" he'd whispered.

Heather had frowned. "Did you say gun?"

Nicky had huddled closer to Joey. Their two swarthy faces with their identical black cowlicks and their identical, conspiratorial glances had gotten to her.

"Nicky, you know how I feel about guns, even toy guns—" Heather had begun.

"You sure you don't want a stuffed rabbit?" Joey had suggested.

"Yuck."

"Well, soldier, I don't want to go against your mother... especially on our honeymoon. She has obviously given this way more thought than I have. So—I can't promise anything before she and I talk about it."

That Nicky had glared at her over Joey's wide shoulder without arguing further as he usually did, confused her. Joey was incredibly supportive and talented with the little boy. The dangerous fantasy of having a mature man share the burden of parenting was too appealing to consider. Whatever she did, she couldn't allow herself to surrender to girlish dreams.

Her pulse throbbed unevenly. Trapped beside Joey in the plane, again she recalled the night Ben had died.

Ben had been driving Julia and Joey and Heather home from a dance. When a cop had chased them, Ben had let everybody out except himself, promising to come back when he lost the patrol car.

But he never had. They'd stood beside that gravel road for an hour before they'd heard the sirens and then rushed toward the sound only to find Ben's bright red car smashed to pieces.

Ben had died protecting Joey and her from their parents. She had blamed herself and Joey for her brother's death.

Giving up Joey had been her atonement.

Her pregnancy had magnified her parents' grief over Ben. They'd been painfully thrilled when she'd lost the baby. Even happier when they'd convinced her to give up Joey. She'd barely known what she was doing. Her only thought had been to ease their grief.

For years she'd tried not to think of Joey or his feelings.

A shiver of apprehension raced through her. It was impossible for her to ignore him when his presence charged the air with so many electric currents she could barely breathe.

Besides forcing her to marry him, what had he ever done to hurt her?

He had loved her. It wasn't his fault he was Deo Fasano's son.

Ever since Joey had become famous, she'd believed his pop image—that he was a trashy, womanizing movie star.

But was he?

He had saved her.

Memories of what Larry had nearly done were coming clearer. She had screamed, and Joey had been there.

Odd, that she had been uptight about sex for years, that she'd fought Larry and then that same night seduced Joey.

Whether she wanted them or not, she had feelings for Joey that she had had for no one else.

Raw masculinity emanated from him. Heather swallowed. Seeking to distract herself, she leaned away from Joey and looked out the window. As the Learjet shot toward the runway like a speeding dart, Las Vegas lit up the desert floor like a galaxy of gaudy stars.

Vegas.

She loathed the shallow sorts of experiences the glittery city stood for—gambling, easy women, meaningless sex—addictive-compulsive behavior, the very things that would most appeal to a womanizer.

She froze as the threatening shapes of the huge hotels grew larger and brighter.

Vegas. The very idea of him making their honeymoon so public in this city not known for wholesome values made her seeth all over again.

Fun fact—he was her husband—until he tired of her. As the big hotels came into sharper focus, the cubist MGM, the Mirage, and then the pyramidal Luxor, the strip of ostentatious buildings blurred into sickening blaze of neon.

Suddenly she was back in Texas in that wedding chapel

with the helicopters whirling outside. Again she was walking down the aisle in her long trailing gown. Again an elegant Joey was turning slowly while Nicky danced up and down so excitedly the rings on his white satin pillow jiggled. Again the smoldering light in Joey's gaze made her spine prickle.

Again, Nicky whirled, his high excitement uncontainable. At the sight of his mother's blushing face half hidden behind a white wedding veil, a slow, bold grin spread across his awestruck face. His devil-may-care smile was so like Joey's, she'd nearly fainted.

When she'd continued to walk stiffly up that plush carpet that muffled her footsteps to the beaming pair with their identical black cowlicks and grins, Nicky had grabbed a wad of her silk skirt and wrapped an arm possessively around Joey's black trouser leg. With a tug he'd dragged them closer to the altar.

Someone—her father, she thought—exhaled a hissing breath of disapproval directly behind them.

Then in that silent church, before the scowling Reverend Scott could begin, her precious little boy's voice had rung to the rafters, "Mom, are you marrying him because he's my real dad?"

Joey's mouth had twisted harshly. Reverend Scott's jaw had slackened. Julia had cried out as two reporters dashed outside.

Pivoting, her face feverish, Heather had seen her father's purple face as he got to his feet. But it was Julia, her eyes overbright as she studied Joey, who most terrified Heather. Then Nellie yanked Travis back down, and Julia smiled wanly.

"Heather," Joey pleaded, extending his strong, brown hand toward her. "Marry me." The pain in his black eyes seared her, tempting her to all the wild mischief that had lain dormant in her heart till she'd seen him on Oscar night. "Please, darling. Don't leave me again—"

As if she could.

An expectant hush mushroomed in that tiny chapel. Outside helicopter rotors roared rhythmically and sirens wailed.

Her heart had beat wildly as she slowly flexed and unflexed her fingers. She forgot that she was humiliating her father and thought only of Joey. In that awkward, never-ending moment of communal quiet when she'd seemed to hesitate before taking Joey's hand, every nerve she'd possessed had screamed Nicky's question, too.

Are you marrying him because he's my real dad?

She'd felt herself hurtling over some fatal abyss, unable to stop herself. This was far worse than when she'd watched Big Duke bolt toward town dragging her pink doll's trunk.

Paralyzed before friends and family, she'd clung to Joey's warm hand when he'd knelt to Nicky's level, rasping *yes* so low only the boy could hear. Then Joey had gravely pressed a long, tanned finger to the little boy's lips as if to seal them. Nicky nodded shyly, his damp fingers tightening on her skirt.

When Joey had stood up again, ridiculous tears had streamed down her cheeks. Joey had squeezed her hand. When he'd brought it to his lips, closed his eyes, and kissed each fingertip with infinite gentleness, the congregation had sobbed too.

She'd felt a thousand eyes boring into her spine as he lifted their joined hands. She felt a thousand hearts willing their marriage.

But it was the memory of Joey's black lashes, so tightly shut when he'd kissed her fingers and Nicky's radiant face that had gotten her through the ceremony.

Somehow she had numbly stumbled through her vows, hardly hearing the preacher icily command Joey to kiss the bride.

She had stiffened when Joey's fingers lifted her veil. But the minute he had touched her, she'd gone limp. Then his strong arms had gathered her close, holding her so fiercely he'd bruised her ribs. After that, he'd shut his eyes. His hard mouth had claimed hers in an endless, glorious kiss.

Slowly her hands climbed his chest and wound around his neck. They must've kissed for a whole minute. Finally, Joey had released her, his eyelids fluttering slowly open to stare deeply into her gaze.

Then he lifted Nicky high in his arms, grabbed her hand, and triumphantly the trio marched out of the chapel.

Nobody had been able to get that sizzling kiss out of their minds. At the wedding reception, Heather's cheeks had flamed from the covert stares and unspoken questions of her friends and family. Everybody was dying to ask about her sudden and inexplicable change of grooms. Not that that was necessary after Nicky's question. Her parents, usually so sociable, barely spoke. Julia wandered about like a ghost. Only Nicky and Mac were at ease.

The first questions Nicky asked were, ''Mom, how come you kissed Joey so long? Can you breathe and kiss at the same time?''

''Not now, darling.''

''What's a honeymoon?''

''I said not now.''

''Then when?''

Mac joined them before Nicky could burst forth with more questions. ''Great champagne. You should have a glass, Heather.''

''I don't feel like celebrating.''

''I do!'' Nicky shouted. ''I've got a daddy now!''

''Only one sip, young man.''

Mac shot her a glance when Nicky bolted more than a sip and then ran off to join his grandparents who were alone in a dark corner. ''Half the single women in the world would cut off their right arm to be you.''

''My family will never forgive me.''

''How come you married Joey then?''

"Would you believe…blackmail?"

Mac's eyes widened speculatively. "No. You don't look like the kind of girl even Joey can push around." Mac leaned closer. "You want to know what I think?"

"I'm not at all sure I do."

"You married each other because you can't stand life without each other. You're just too stubborn to admit it."

"My family hates him."

"They don't really know him."

"They think he's a womanizer…like his father."

"They're wrong."

No sooner had Mac said this than she saw Joey surrounded by her bridesmaids. His black head was thrown back, muscles rippling tightly beneath his tuxedo as he laughed. His bevy of admirers giggled and stared at him with huge, adoring eyes.

In high school, she'd been the popular one. Well, the tables had turned.

Dagger-sharp pain splintered her heart. "He doesn't need a wife. He's got a harem."

"You're jealous…*because* you love him."

"I don't care who he flirts with. The more the merrier."

"You don't need to worry about him with other women. He can't be a movie star every second of his life. He's a man. He loves you. The sooner you two stop fooling yourselves and making each other miserable, the better. He loves you. Period. When you believe that simple truth, you won't have to be jealous no matter who he flirts with."

"Please!"

"Believe me," Mac said. "If anybody knows the hell Joey Fasano's been through the past few years, it's me. He needs you. More than you know." He paused and then finished softly, "More than *he* knows."

Heather scarcely heard him. She was watching Joey, noting how alive he seemed, more alive than any other man in the room. The air around him seemed charged as he flirted and the girls laughed. More girls joined the original group.

He was like a sexual magnet.

Watching them, Heather's heart filled with pain.

How could she possibly hold on to him when every woman on earth wanted him?

Eight

Heather pressed splayed fingers against the tiny oval window of the jet. "Oh, no, Joey—"

Motorcycles were zooming toward their plane like a band of marauding Comanches. Heather gasped. The Learjet had barely stopped before at least half a dozen paparazzi had them surrounded.

Joey hunched closer, bristling as the mob swelled between the jet and their waiting limo. Then he jumped up and grabbed her elbow. "Babe, we've gotta get out of here—fast."

"Now?"

"It won't get easier. More'll come, I swear. We've got to get off this damn plane."

"This is your fault!"

Ignoring her, he rushed her toward the exit, shouting to the crew to bring their luggage later. In the next instant, the steps were down, and they stood outside above the noisy crowd in a warm, opalescent twilight. When the reporters beneath them clambered up a few steps and began screaming questions, Joey's protective arm circled her.

"Kiss her!" they yelled.

"On one condition," Joey said, adoring his bride with his famous, devil-may-care smile.

They waited.

"You get your picture—then you leave us alone to enjoy our honeymoon."

As the reporters nodded in unison, Joey tightened his hands around her waist, shaping her slim body to his length. When her shocked gaze flew to his face, a muscle flickered in his hard jawline.

"I don't really think they'll leave us alone," he confessed, "but, hell, anything's worth a try. Besides, I've been wanting to kiss you the whole time you've been arguing."

She smiled weakly, on his side this once since they faced a common enemy.

As Joey deliberately drew out the moment before their kiss, her traitorous heart sped up. Every nerve in her being came alive when he closed his eyes, his hand slowly stroking her slender throat. His touch was as gentle and tactile as a blind man's. As always with his eyes shut, his face was as innocent as an angel's. In that long instant before their lips met and hundreds of flashbulbs exploded, she seemed to stop breathing. She closed her eyes, too, and forgot the hundred or so fans and reporters streaming around their limousine.

It was as if in that suspended, magical moment, time stood still and they were the only two people on earth. As if despite the millions of women who adored him and the reporters struggling to climb the metal stairs, she was the only woman who would ever really matter to him.

Then his hot mouth found hers, and she felt a warmly delicious quiver go through her. Flashes exploded. He was probably used to doing love scenes for a film crew. Her response was so immediate and devastatingly personal, she resented him for publicly staging what should have been a private act. This was putting on a show. He was acting.

She wasn't. And that made her furious.

As his fingers played with the springy ringlets that lay damply against her neck, Heather ripped herself from him and tore down the steps. Before he could stop her, she plunged wildly into the clamoring throng.

Joey screamed her name and leapt after her.

A mob with raised notepads and microphones fell on her like jackals.

"Miss Wade— Miss Wade—"

"Who's Nicky?"

"Is he the reason Joey Fasano married you?"

"What did the kid say in church?"

She turned white and stumbled. As she fell into their frenzied midst, she screamed. Just before she hit the ground, Joey yanked her up into his strong arms. A fan grabbed a handful of her hair and pulled hard. Another hand ripped her skirt. Her sweater was pulled half off her shoulder. Stubby fingers with long nails scratched her chest and closed around her necklace. Women screamed for Joey and tore at his clothes and hair, too.

Heather wept frantically. Joey was shoving and pushing them both toward the limo, but the gauntlet seemed endless. She felt dizzy, unable to stand as the fans' screams pulsated. If Joey hadn't protected her, they would have stripped her naked.

Then Louie was there, barging into the crowd, running interference with his linebacker's body so that Joey could carry her safely through the crunch of overexcited fans.

A redhead ripped off her bra from under her T-shirt and jammed it into Joey's hand. "Wanna D-cup?"

A reporter yelled, "What does Senator Wade think about your love child?"

Even when Heather was inside the limo, fists kept pound-

ing on the windows. More reporters yelled questions.
Heather became aware of Joey's bloody face and torn shirt.
A thin line of red streamed from a small gash above his
eyebrow.

Dear God. Joey looked like he'd fought a war. Would
her life with him always be this insane? Or would it get
worse?

There was a fierce new violence in his face. When he
glared at her, she began to shake.

"What?" she demanded in a low, throbbing voice. Then
she saw the white straps dripping out of his bruised hand
and realized he was holding some woman's huge bra.

"Oh, my God," she whispered in disgust. "How could
you do this to me? To my family? To Nicky?"

"Don't ever do something like that again," he growled,
pitching the bra onto the floorboard.

"Oh, so it's my fault?"

"Yes, you little fool." His taut voice shook nearly as
much as hers did. "Don't you understand? They almost
knocked you down. They could have crushed you, killed
you."

"You were the one who staged that kiss. Did you do
that to embarrass my father?"

"Forget him for once in your damned life. This isn't
about him. This is about us. About you. About our life.
They could have hurt you." He paused. "And you never
know. There could be a guy, a kidnapper, a crazy fan, a
terrorist...some weirdo who's just pretending to be a journalist. As a senator's daughter, you should know this
stuff."

Kidnapper. The word burned into her mind, into her soul.
An eerie tingle swept her as she remembered Trevor Pilot
and her brush with pure evil two years ago. He'd threatened
Nicky, threatened her. For a while she'd been afraid of
every stranger, of her own shadow even.

"D-don't be ridiculous," she said, turning her face away.

''You listen to me. I know what I'm saying. These photographers are relentless. They've got their jobs to do. But we've got our lives to live. If we let them get too close, they'll invade our private life.''

''You staged that kiss.''

''So—we were above them. Safe.''

''I don't think I'll ever feel safe again. Not as long as I'm married to you.''

''And you prize safety?''

''More than anything.''

''Right. Then why were you gonna marry a guy who tried to rape you?''

A compulsive shudder ran through her.

She wanted to say he was wrong, but he wasn't. Larry was another example of her bad decisions.

She'd loved Joey. She'd chosen a dangerous career that had put her child in harm's way.

She squeezed her eyes shut. She'd been trying so hard to be good. How had her life spun so crazily out of control—again?

''You're married to me,'' Joey said.

''If only, if only, I could forget that bitter fact.''

''I have no intention, none whatsoever, of ever letting you do that.'' His voice was soft and yet biting and cynical, too. ''This is our honeymoon—remember?''

''This isn't a real marriage. We aren't going to have a real honeymoon, either. Not in this ridiculous city.''

''Don't bet on it.''

Her eyes popped open. When he grinned, his white teeth made his sun-browned skin seem even darker. She turned her face to the window.

More flashbulbs went off. Blinded, she buried her face in her hands on a sob.

Behind her fingers, more flashes whitened the tinted windows.

''Vegas is hell, and you're the devil.''

The air between them had developed a thickness. For a moment she thought she'd hurt him.

Then Joey threw back his head and roared with laughter.

"So—I'm the devil. Well, you're no saint. You're just afraid of the fun we'll have when I tempt you to wanton wickedness."

"Don't mock me."

She felt his hand move across leather and touch the back of her neck. Joey's voice was strangely quiet. "I won't...but you've got to stop baiting me and blaming me for everything first."

"But—" She was determined to sulk. "You deserve to be unhappy."

"And you don't?" His carved features remained expressionless. Even so, she heard the hint of a smile beginning in his voice. "Am I right?"

"You're exactly right—for once," she acquiesced.

"You're perfect?" he murmured.

His husky tone made her nerves jump.

"Compared to you—"

He snorted. "You dump me. For six damn years you don't say a thing about Nicky. And I'm the big villain. Sorry, sweetheart, that script wouldn't wash in Hollywood."

"I wanted you out of my life."

"You were damned selfish. Lucky for you, I've a forgiving nature." He loosened his tie and lay back, sprawling across the plush leather seats. He closed his eyes.

Dark shadows lay beneath those curved, black lashes. He looked so beat suddenly and yet so innocent, too, her heart almost softened. But the virile earthiness of his blatant, male sexuality made her feminine senses catapult in alarm.

Alone with him, she was on dangerous ground.

"I can't believe this is happening."

"Believe it. I'm back to stay," he said, opening his eyes. "You had things your way for six damn years." His voice was cold. "Now it's my turn." He stared past her out the window.

They sped along with a fleet of motorcycles roaring behind them. At first she was too angry with him to notice that Vegas pulsed with a life of its own. Louie made no attempt to lose the swarm, maybe because he didn't want to endanger anybody.

The strip was clogged with shiny, fast cars; the sidewalks jammed with fat, lumbering tourists.

When they swerved toward the hotel, a throng of bellhops mobbed their limousine. As he got out, Joey slid on a pair of sunglasses.

Flashbulbs exploded. Journalists screamed questions. Fans begged for autographs.

Joey took Heather's hand.

"We hate you, Heather," a group of women chorused. "You stole our love-man."

Joey laced his fingers through hers. "Look straight in front of you." Then quickly he hurried Heather inside a wonderland of fake, white marble columns that soared seven stories above an opulent casino decorated with naked, golden statues, and long, blue reflecting pools. Ivies dripped from marble balconies. Inside, an army of security guards charged them and held the press and fans at bay. For a moment, remembering the incident at the airport, Heather felt dizzy with fear that she would be crushed in the stampede.

But Joey's arms stayed around her. His reassuring voice murmured behind her ear. "It's okay, babe."

A dark-haired beauty in a sari behind the reception desk waved them toward a bank of elevators. "Show Mr. Fasano to his private elevator. Penthouse A." She held her hands up and clapped. "Now. Before everybody sees him and goes wild."

Fame. Maybe that was what charged the air around Joey

with baffling heat and wound-up emotion. She'd always
thought it was just Joey.

Swiftly Joey led Heather along the edge of the plush
casino where slot machines jingled as coins plunked noisily
into tin trays. Two Elvis impersonators in white sequined
capes rushed past them.

Just as she and Joey reached the elevators, a dark-
skinned platinum blonde tore Joey from Heather.

"I love you, baby," she cooed in a honeyed voice that
was deep and dark and edgily erotic. "I'd do anything—
anything for you, baby." She slipped something into his
pocket.

Heather's mind played a trick. The blonde turned into a
silver octopus. Then a green fog blinded Heather, and she
rushed blindly toward the elevators.

"Not now," Joey replied as Louie peeled the lady off
him.

Flashbulbs popped.

Heather dabbed at her wet, burning eyes with the back
of her hand. Her body shook convulsively as she punched
every button in the elevator. The doors were slamming
when Joey reached them. Through the slit in the doors, their
gazes locked for an endless second.

"Heather! Open—"

At his taut expression, dizzying weakness spread through
her. Then his dusky face blurred in waves of green.

Heather punched her fist hard on the close-door button
just as Joey rammed his foot sideways between the doors.

"Ouch!"

The bronze doors bounced off his foot, and he limped
inside. His sheepish expression was a silent apology.

Not good enough.

Heather felt helpless and humiliated that a scantily
clothed stranger had thrown herself at *her* husband right
there in front of her. As if she hadn't even existed.

"Don't pretend you didn't enjoy that."

"I'm sorry," he said quietly.

She forced what she hoped was a nonchalant smile, but, of course, it wasn't. "Why? Women like her are your perks. I'm sure you love them all."

"Okay. *Fine.*" His angry gaze narrowed on her stricken face briefly. But the look was long enough for her to see that he was now seething with as much hostility as she. As if he considered *her* attack unfair. "I won't argue," he said tightly.

The quick flash of pain that came and went in his eyes shocked her. She didn't want to feel remorse, but the emotion that twisted her heart was very close to it. She almost swayed into him, almost extended a hand to offer him a silent apology. Almost. But not quite. Jealousy and pride— the memory of their humiliating wedding, the staged kiss— all these things and more stopped her.

A mask crept over his features, carving them with new hardness. Neither of them spoke, so the tension thickened as their tiny elevator whizzed them like two wild animals trapped in the same cage to his lavish penthouse.

Everybody wants to be me, she thought.

Everybody except me.

Not once did Heather look at Joey. She stepped haughtily past him only to gasp in disgust at the tasteless, garish vulgarity of the penthouse. Red carpet and gilt-framed mirrors were everywhere—on the walls, on the ceilings, above every velvet couch, above every massive bed.

Golden, naked statues in lewd postures adorned every red staircase.

She whirled on him indignantly. "Oh, no—" she cried. "This looks like the perfect setting for an orgy."

"It's our honeymoon suite," he said innocently.

"It's a bordello."

"Which makes it perfect...for our purposes."

"Maybe for *your* purposes."

"You got it, babe."

"You are the devil."

He stared at her, his hot gaze running over her face and body. "Then take something off and inspire me to fiendish mischief."

"Joey, please."

One wickedly arched black eyebrow mocked her. "You wouldn't have liked any hotel I picked. So, I thought, why not push a few of your buttons...just for the fun?" He paused. "There's a fine line between your temper and your passion. Sometimes one leads straight to the other. I thought I might as well give it a try."

She flushed. The rest of her body did a slow burn as she realized the sunken pools, the hot tubs, the velvet couches and the red satin beds had been chosen to seduce her.

Joey's languid, too-knowing eyes sent tingles up her spine. "Getting hungry, babe?"

"For what?" she snapped.

He laughed. "That's my wanton woman." He winked. "Supper can wait, then—while we enjoy...each other."

"No. I didn't mean—"

"Did you know that if you eat...your blood goes to your stomach to aid digestion...instead of to other...more important parts of your anatomy?"

"I—I'm starving," she inserted quickly.

"For me." He was now standing mere inches behind her.

She jumped away as he began jerking his tie through his collar.

"What are you doing?"

He yanked off his jacket. "What does it look like? This is our wedding night. Last night you were as hot as a firecracker. I was hoping this place and a little friendly persuasion might inspire you to top that thrilling performance."

"Would you hush with the sex talk?"

His black eyes ignored her fear. "Not likely."

"Don't do this, Joey. And...and put your tie back on."

"Only if you promise to come over here and undress me yourself."

"I said quit that."

"I was hoping that if I stripped, you'd feel inspired to do the same."

"Joey!"

He gave her a sidelong look. "Really, would it kill you to put on something more comfortable?"

"How many times have you said that to other women?"

He smiled broadly, imperturbably. "Never—to my wife."

Even though she didn't look at him, she grew jittery as his unwavering gaze continued to study her.

"As if our sham of a marriage makes all this so special," she challenged.

"It does." He paused meaningfully. "You are. To me."

The intensity in his voice made her stomach flutter.

Don't believe him. He's not really part of your life. He brought you to this ridiculous place.

"I don't believe you," she said.

He shrugged. "Suit yourself. Just get undressed—"

"You could have anybody. That woman who threw herself at you—she thinks you're a god."

The room went so utterly silent, Heather was certain she could have heard a dust mote fall.

"I know," he said.

"To me you're a real man, a mere mortal."

"Good," he declared.

"Good?"

His smile was strained. "Heather, what do I have to say? Or do? I married you, didn't I?" He came toward her. "I'm *your* husband." Reaching for her, he put his hands on her shoulders. She hated the way her skin flamed beneath his fingers. "Women like her mean nothing to me. I'm an actor. I play parts."

"Are you playing one now?"

Slowly he lifted his gaze to her face. "No," he said in that husky undertone that could melt a million hearts. "Women like her fall in love with the tough guys I play. They don't know *me*. You do. I'm sick and tired of phony relationships. I want something *real*."

"Is that what you call this place—real?"

"No. But you're real...to me."

She squeezed her hands over her ears and closed her eyes, as she'd done years ago when they were kids to shut him out when he'd been obnoxious.

"Look," he said. "I'm sorry." The intensity in his gaze made her catch her breath. "You know how I used to get carried away when it came to pranks. I just thought maybe you still had a sense of humor."

"You used to devil me when I was already mad enough to spit nails."

"I know." Again that broad sheepish grin of his. "You'd get hopping mad. But most times we'd end up in bed."

"Later we laughed till we cried."

"We had such fun. Maybe that's why I couldn't help myself—"

"You're awful," she accused. "Incorrigible."

He nodded.

"A devil—in the flesh," she said, but this time without malice.

"Now be honest, isn't that the best kind of devil... I mean if you were the judge of a devil contest?"

Her lips were twitching at the corners. "So, you brought me here just to make me mad?"

"Or to make you laugh." His grin was quick and charming. "Mostly to get you into bed."

In spite of herself, her eyes sparkled with some of that old delight. Her cheeks glowed.

He caught her face in his hands. "Do you have any idea what it does to me when you look at me like that?" His voice was rough. His dark eyes went wide. "I've never forgotten you. I wanted to. Oh, God, Heather, how I wanted to."

She swallowed, as torn as he. "I wanted to forget you, too."

For years she'd told herself everybody would be better off if she forgot him. She'd be the *good* daughter. The *good* mother.

But now that she was alone with Joey, he seemed so different from the womanizer in the tabloids. He seemed like Joey. Just Joey. *Her* Joey.

"It's too late to go back," she whispered. "Our lifestyles are totally incompatible."

"I thought so, too. Then Roth tried to rape you. I went berserk. You seduced me."

"No."

"Things happen. Things you don't choose. And suddenly everything looks different. I can't explain it. I had feelings I didn't know—"

"I didn't know what I was doing."

He was shaking his black head. "Maybe. Like I said, things happen. Things you don't choose. Maybe last night was the first honest step either one of us has taken in years. Maybe I've been looking for happiness the wrong way while you've been so busy making everybody else happy, you forgot yourself."

"I'm confused."

"You threw yourself at me like you were starving."

"I told you. I didn't know what I was doing."

"Maybe it's time you found out." His intense dark stare made her feel weak.

"You attach way too much importance to sex."

"Yeah. I do. It's a fault."

"One of many," she said.

He pulled her closer, pressing her face into his warm,

broad chest, so that she heard and felt the steady, heavy thumping of his heart beneath her ear.

"Make love to me, Heather. Make love to me like you did last night. It felt good. Right."

"It was wrong."

"Maybe."

He lifted her chin, turned her face to his. She reached up and covered his hand with her own.

As always the least physical contact set off a chain reaction in both of them.

Nevertheless, she was determined to resist him. She held herself absolutely still. But, as always, her body had a secret will all its own. Hardly knowing what she did, she began to move. First, her arms slid underneath his shirt and circled his lean waist. With a shiver, he drew her nearer. Lifting his shirttails, with lips that were desperate to taste him, she knelt and kissed the hard, warm skin as if she could never get enough of him.

"Joey, oh, Joey—" she breathed, clasping her hands together at the small of his muscular back, kissing him, dying inside, surrendering completely to an instinct that was too true to deny.

The tension drained out of him. His arms came around her. His feverish mouth burned through her hair into her scalp.

Just as he lifted her into his arms, a knock pounded jarringly against their door.

Startled, she jerked free. Still, for a long moment she couldn't tear her gaze from his face. "Heather," he whispered. Then his eyes released hers, and he strode angrily toward the door to let the bellmen in with their luggage.

Shaken, her heart racing, she ran to the long windows, parted the drapes, and looked out at the sparkling city.

Then the bellhops were gone, and they were alone again.

Joey started toward her. She released the curtain with a snap and backed away. Sensing her new mood, he went to the bar and splashed brandy into a crystal glass. "Care to join me?" he offered, lifting his glass.

"Sure." Her uneven pulse belied her casual tone as he approached her with the drink.

She took it hastily, but their hands brushed, sparking more raw emotions. She jerked her glass to her lips, sloshing brandy onto the red carpet.

With one hand he unbuttoned his torn shirt, exposing more virile, brown neck and lean torso. He ripped the shredded garment all the way off. Without his shirt, jacket and tie, he looked less civilized, more dangerously male.

Wanting to rid herself of the taste of him and the sight of so many ripply muscles, she whirled, gulping her brandy so fast she choked.

"Careful," he warned. "You're a better kisser than you are a drinker."

"I know what I'm doing," she whispered on a strangled note.

"Do you?"

Defiantly she tossed the rest of her glass down.

Big mistake. In the next instant it was burning her esophagus, choking her. The room was swirling.

"Hey, hey," he whispered treading soundlessly closer.

"So help me, touch me again, and I'll kill you—"

"Like you did a while ago?" His know-it-all grin was as cocky as ever even as his soft, rough voice beguiled her. "You were the one who got things heated up last night."

"I want to forget that—"

"Maybe you do." He moved still closer. "I don't."

She shrieked, trying to jump away, but he was faster. Catching her to him, he wound his hand through her hair, reeling her nearer. "Maybe it's my turn to seduce you."

"No."

"Heather, are you going to hate me forever?"

"If possible."

"Is this any way to start a marriage?"

"You should have thought of that when you forced me to marry you."

His fingers tensed as he dragged her face to his. "You might have married that creep—"

"His name is Larry."

"He's a creep."

Dark, terrifying images of Larry pressing her down onto the bed rose in her imagination.

"Why would you care?"

"I care." Under his breath, he said, "I don't know why. But I just couldn't risk losing you or Nicky to him. The thought of him touching you makes me crazy."

"You're no better than Larry. You're forcing me—"

"Compared to that guy, I'm a saint."

"You're no saint."

"I said compared to—" Joey grinned. "Hey. Just listen to us. This conversation is inane. I feel like I've been waiting for my life to start for six damn years. We're here in sexy digs, and we keep talking at each other. Neither one of us is making a damn bit of sense. You're married to me, Heather. For better or worse. We have Nicky. This is our wedding night—"

"Don't remind me."

"Shut up and let me kiss you."

He gripped the bottom edges of her sweater. Before she knew what he had in mind, he'd flipped it over her head.

"Don't—"

Just as deftly he unhooked her bra.

Her breasts swung free. Her body burned under his gaze.

"You're my woman. Why don't you act like it?"

"Joey," she whispered.

"You're so damned beautiful," he said. "Nobody comes close."

He knelt before her and cupped her breasts. He moved his tongue slowly across each nipple until they peaked beneath his lips.

"Tell me you don't want me now—"

"I—I don't." But the wanton sigh she expelled told a different story.

"You're mine." His words were low and thick, his kisses hot. "All mine."

She wanted him to kiss her like that for a long time, to explore every part of her with his mouth, but she was determined to fight him, too. Even as his hands shaped her body to his and tingles of desire spiraled through her when he kissed her, she managed a last, shaky protest. "Marriage isn't about sex. You don't love me."

He froze. "Why the hell should I?" he said softly.

His hands and mouth ceased to move. She swallowed hard. Some part of her still wanted him to strip her, to make wild, passionate love to her.

Instead he let her go. "Love?" His eyes were hot and dark with the same ravaged pain she'd seen Oscar night. "I loved you, and you threw me out. I let you go. I stayed away because I loved you. Damn you, Heather. I was a stupid, young fool. I don't want your love...ever again. I want your body. Our kid. I'm willing to be faithful. I'm willing to try to get along. But do me a favor and don't ever say that word again. You taught me that love is a false religion. Or a drug I no longer choose to be hooked on. You thrill me in bed. Period." His hard gaze made her feel cold and empty.

"Then I'm your whore. Not your wife."

"No. That's not the way it is," he said in a low, dead tone, backing away from her. "But there will be conditions to this marriage." He gathered up his shirt, buttoned it, and raked a shaking hand through his long black hair.

"Marriage means total commitment," she whispered.

He grabbed his tie. "You're a fine one to talk, babe."

"Joey—"

"You think I don't want all those things? You think I don't want a real marriage?" He paused. "You taught me I couldn't ever have them."

He slammed the door and was gone.

Nine

When hearts tear, they make no sound.

She should know that by now.

Joey had been gone an hour, and Heather was still dazed and reeling from the hurt.

The only noise in the vast penthouse besides the drumming beat of that lifeless organ inside her breast was the merciless ticking of a golden clock adorned with cupids that squatted on the mantel.

On a shuddering breath, Heather stared at the lewd cupids and then at the door and then at Joey's discarded jacket on the plush, red carpet, but the image that burned in her mind and made her ache was Joey's stark, haunted features.

She saw his wild black hair falling uncombed over that slim gash above his brow. Saw his sensual mouth compressed in pain. Saw the shadows of exhaustion beneath his empty eyes. Saw new lines carved deeper into brown flesh. Saw the slump of his broad, proud shoulders.

Why wasn't she wild with relief that he was gone?

She didn't want his love.

Why then did she fall to her knees and pick up his jacket? She'd buried her face in the soft wool, inhaled his scent, kissed the expensive fabric, remembered the warmth of his hands on her skin. It was an act of worship and defeat.

Unbidden came memories of the aggressive blonde who'd thrown herself at Joey. Next Heather remembered Daniella's gorgeous face and perfect body.

Joey could have anybody.

He'd married her.

Her father said Joey was a worthless, shallow womanizer, like Deo.

I won't cheat. Believe it.

Joey had sworn fidelity to her even more fiercely than he'd sworn never to love her.

You think I don't want a real marriage.

Her throat tightened. She tossed his jacket down and stood up. She didn't want his love. She didn't want this marriage. She didn't want anything from him. She wanted to forget how passionately he'd once adored her. Because if she remembered then she might have to—

She might have to face what she'd done to him.

She'd hurt him.

I loved you, and you threw me out. I let you go, I stayed away, because I loved you.

She hadn't wanted to know that. Hadn't wanted to think about him—ever. A girl still, she'd been ashamed of her sexuality, of her young passionate feelings, of sneaking out to date Joey, of getting pregnant when she wasn't married. She'd been so consumed by Joey, she hadn't cared about anything except him, not even Ben, till he died. Thus, when their world had come crashing down, she'd thought that if she hadn't been so in love, so blind to her family's needs, maybe she could have seen the disaster coming and somehow prevented it.

Maybe she'd blamed herself and Joey unfairly for Ben's death. She'd foolishly thought if she sacrificed Joey, she could make everything all right.

But nothing had ever gone right since. Maybe that wrong turning was what had brought the rest—all the crazy boyfriends, even Larry, her inability to cope with the dangers of her career, her terror of life going really wrong again, the need for a safe, sane marriage—

Maybe her sacrifice, like most sacrifices, had been stupid and ill-conceived. She no longer felt ashamed of her teenage romance. She felt lucky to have known such love.

Accidents happen. They hurt terribly. Too often scapegoats must be found by guilt-ridden survivors.

Joey had loved Ben, too.

She'd never written him; never called. She'd hung up on him that one time he'd called her. Maybe she'd worked so hard to put Joey out of her mind because she'd been running from her own conscience.

She'd been everything to Joey. His father had been a drunken lout who'd beat him, his mother a silent victim too terrorized to defend him. Then Ben had died. Julia had run away. And Heather had abandoned him.

Was it any wonder Joey didn't want love?

As a boy he'd been so open and tenderhearted. His need for love had been huge. Who besides her had ever been there for him? When he'd lost his best friend and his sister, who had consoled him? Who was there for him now? What did he have besides money and fame? If such things were soul-satisfying, why on Oscar night, had he said she was unforgettable? Why had his doing so scared her so deeply?

He'd saved her from date rape.

They'd made love.

She hadn't gone to bed with anybody else—ever.

For six years her life had been on hold.

So had his.

Why?

Joey had said that seducing him was the first honest step she'd taken in six years.

Suddenly she wished him back. She wanted his hands and mouth on her skin. She wanted to lie quivering beneath his caressing hands. She wanted him inside her, their bodies joined, his lips crying her name as he lost himself and his pain in her embrace.

But he wasn't coming back.

Slowly, like one wakening from a trance, she stumbled toward the door. She wanted to rush out of the penthouse, to find him before he found some other woman, to beg him to forgive her.

No. She couldn't go after him. This had to be some strange mood that possessed her. This was her chance to be free of him, to make her family happy.

If you don't make yourself happy, how can you possibly make anyone else happy?

Defiantly, she flung open the door. Louie snapped to attention when he saw her white face and wild eyes. When she ran past him, the bodyguard raced down the long hall after her.

Downstairs the huge casino was a beehive of humming slot machines, roulette wheels, and crap tables. Gamblers with weathered faces and cigarettes dripping from their mouths guzzled highballs from plastic glasses as they mindlessly cranked the slots. Others screamed numbers, still others put their yellowed fingertips together and prayed to that unpredictable god of all gamblers before they crouched low over tables and pitched dice.

But no Joey.

When Heather whirled around, Louie's eyes bulged.

"Where is he?" she whispered.

Watery eyes rolled in his big, dark face. "He wants to be alone."

"Where?"

He hesitated. Then without speaking, he motioned her to

follow him out of the casino, through a maze of hallways to a private VIP bar. He inserted a card into a slot in the wall.

Cracking the door a couple of inches, he pointed. ''He looks like a lost soul, don't he?''

Across the smoky darkness a tall, black-haired man was hunched over a mahogany bar. He held a bottle of brandy in one hand and a half-filled glass in the other. Behind him a black man played blues on a grand piano.

Joey's dark face was so savage and so filled with regret, Heather wanted to die. She gasped and then brought a shaking hand to her mouth. But Joey whirled on that muted, unguarded sound, and pinned her with a wild black stare.

She saw shock and disbelief in his eyes. Then his face hardened.

He half rose, shoving his barstool aside before he took a fierce step toward her.

On a strangled sob, she ran—out the door, into the casino, charging straight into a paunchy gambler carrying a cup full of quarters and a beer.

Quarters and beer spewed everywhere.

''Hey! Watch where you're going, girlie.''

Blindly, she dashed toward the elevators. Louie was right behind her.

Before she let herself inside the penthouse, she put a hand on Louie's arm. ''Thank you for taking me to Joey. I was afraid he might be with…someone—''

Louie stared at her. ''Who?''

''What about all those women.…''

''Women?''

''The ones in the tabloids—''

''Girl, don't you know the stories is mostly lies? He don't chase women. He don't have to.''

''What about that naked girl in his swimming pool?''

''She pulled that stunt to trap him. The truth be—until you—he mostly be alone. And no wonder. Those women may be pretty, but they're after one thing. They wants some of his shine to rub off on them.''

Heather's heart skittered crazily. What had she done?

''Thank you, Louie,'' she murmured.

Inside, she unpacked and put on her nightgown. But when she slipped beneath the satin spread, the bed felt alien. One minute it was too soft; the next too hard. She tossed and twisted. Finally, she just lay there, tangled in those sheets, staring up at her white, lonely reflection in the huge, gilt mirror overhead.

She held her hand up and fingered her gold wedding band. One minute her body trembled, the next it went taut as a bowstring.

She ached with needs, too long repressed. The bed felt cold without Joey. Why had she been such a fool? Joey had had the guts to stand up and thank her before the whole world. He'd saved her from Larry. He'd married her. He hadn't liked the press turning their wedding into a circus any more than she had.

He'd said he wanted them to be a family.

Mrs. Joey Fasano.

Some wife. All she'd done was tear him down.

She felt the crushing despair of someone who knows she'd heedlessly thrown her whole life away...again.

Sitting up stiffly, she plumped her pillow. Just as she was wondering how she would ever get through the night and how she could even begin to sort out her confused feelings, the phone rang.

She grabbed it, her heart trilling expectantly. Maybe *he* would make it easy for her after all.

''I've been watching you.''

It wasn't Joey.

Heather's hand went to her mouth, strangling a scream.

''It's me, Trevor.''

She closed her eyes in fright and despair.

Trevor's coarse, knowing laughter sent a cold shiver through her.

As if it were yesterday she saw his cruel, gray face beneath his filthy growth of beard; again she felt his cold, colorless eyes on her when she'd testified. Somehow he'd formed a weird bond with her, a bond she hadn't wanted.

"They were supposed to lock you up forever," she whispered.

He laughed, and only with the greatest effort did she cling to her self-possession and sanity.

"I saw you on TV. You married that movie star. Your old love. Your kid's daddy. Life's gotten too good for you. How come life's never gotten good for me?"

"Where are you? How did you get this number?"

"You won that big prize for taking my picture. That money is mine, Senator's daughter, movie star's wife. I told you so in those letters you never answered. Your kid's mine. I'll get him, too." Trevor laughed. "Just like I got the ambassador's. Only this time you won't be there snapping pictures. You'll pay big to get him back. I'll be famous."

"Where are you?"

"Where? Where?" he mimicked. "I busted out, that's where. You should've answered my letters. My mother never wrote, either."

"You tell me where," she screamed.

"Say hi to your movie star," he said. "Tell him I'm a big fan. I want that black jacket he wore in *Hellraiser*—along with a suitcase of cash."

"Where—"

"Did I ever tell you, you're even prettier than my mother? You have big sweet eyes, just like she did."

The line went dead.

One minute Joey was grimly swirling brandy in his glass, and the next he saw a familiar golden head backlighted in the doorway.

Heather. His breath came hard. His eyes couldn't stop looking at her. He took an involuntary step toward her.

Self-loathing washed him in those few seconds before she bolted.

She couldn't stand him.

He didn't blame her.

Maybe she'd lied about Nicky six years ago. Maybe she'd mentioned love when he'd been hell-bent on seduction. But what was he doing to her? Forcing her? Threatening her?

He had to get a grip before it was too late. Maybe Travis had been right about him all along. Maybe he was no better than his no-good, judgmental, tyrannical father.

For a second he considered letting her go—again. The world was full of women. Maybe if he looked hard, really searched, he could find someone decent.

Hell.

Been there. Done that. He'd learned the first time his heart wasn't into finding someone else. Maybe he never would be.

Maybe movie stars were supposed to enjoy lots of women jumping them. He didn't. Sex was too big a deal. He couldn't open up to strangers even if they were incredibly beautiful.

Heather was the only woman he seemed to want. In his cabin, she'd turned him to flame. For a few brief moments she'd driven out the darkness and accumulated loneliness of six long years.

He was helpless against her appeal; still, he couldn't force her to stay.

How long he sat there, brooding about freeing her while knowing he could never free himself, he didn't know. But when Joey heard the door and looked up, she was there, her hair catching the light of the golden light, her slim, nervous fingers heating his arm where she hesitantly touched him.

"I'm sorry," she began haltingly in a tone as soft as an angel's.

"No, you were right." His own voice was strangely rough. "I'm the one who's sorry." He saw her tears and his heart constricted.

"Oh, Joey—" she blurted, her burning fingers tightening convulsively on his arm.

Shakily he pulled her closer. Her violet irises were huge; her pupils pinpricks; her muscles rigid. Something was terribly wrong. Instinctively he knew it had nothing to do with him.

"Babe, what is it?"

She shuddered. "It's Nicky. Trevor..."

Joey stared, waiting, needing more. But when she couldn't go on, an odd, terrifying tension began to build inside him.

"Trevor Pilot. He...he called. He's after Nicky this time."

"Trevor?" The name rang a dull, unpleasant bell, but the brandy dulled his brain, and he couldn't place it.

Her wild, staring eyes never blinked.

"It's my fault...for marrying you," she said.

Joey choked back fear. If he wasn't careful, she would fly to pieces.

"What about Nicky? Who's this Trevor?"

His gentleness coupled with the softness of his deep voice broke her resistance. "Pilot." She forced the dreaded name through teeth that chattered. "He called a while ago.... He heard about us. He threatened me."

"I don't understand," Joey said.

"When I won the Pulitzer.... When I—I took that picture in that forest of that man carrying a little boy, I thought I was photographing a loving father and his darling child.

But that picture identified the man as Trevor Pilot. Trevor had kidnapped the English ambassador's only son…''

''I remember.''

Tears filled her eyes. ''When the police found the child, Trevor was crouched over him with a hammer. He'd smashed his hand once. He intended to break every bone in that child's body. I—I made a terrible, crazy enemy.'' She began to cry.

''Your picture was poignant, wonderful. I called you, remember?''

''My life was out of control just like it was when Ben died. I couldn't talk to you or anybody.''

Joey had read the coverage of the trial. Why hadn't he realized—

Joey's arms tightened around her. He let her cling till she quieted.

''I'd been taking pictures of happy events. I thought that picture was a loving picture. It was an accident that it turned out to be what it was, to be so important. I didn't deserve a Pulitzer. Then I had to testify against that…that madman. He made all sorts of crazy threats. He said he'd get me, and he'd get my child. I couldn't deal with my own life much less… Now he's out again.''

''I thought they locked him up.''

''They did, but he got out and he heard about us. Oh, Joey, why do terrible things keep happening to me? Why can't I live a normal life? I gave you up. I quit taking pictures…''

''Shhh. You can't control your life.'' Still, against every instinct, he asked, ''Would it be easier…if I left?''

She broke down completely then. ''Oh, maybe. But… Oh, Joey, this is worse than when Ben died. Worse— I know he's coming after me partly because I'm married to you. If he gets Nicky, it'll make a big splash. That's what he wants—to steal some famous person's child. But…but I can't face this…alone.''

When her eyes could not leave his, his breath came hard. She was asking him to stay.

"There. There," he soothed, holding her till she grew calmer.

Then he lifted his napkin from the bar and wiped the dark smudges of her eyeshadow from beneath her lashes. With equal gentleness he smoothed her tangled hair into some semblance of order.

"Say the word, and I'll go. I'll help from the sidelines. I don't want to make this harder for you."

For an agonized minute she was silent again.

"Joey, oh, Joey. I said I wanted you to stay. Please—"

"All right," he said, determined never again to take advantage of her. "On one condition—"

Except for their shadowy, corner booth, the crowded cafeteria was brightly lit. Joey hadn't bothered to remove their coffee mugs or their buttered toast from their plastic trays. He'd chosen the booth because it offered privacy.

She hadn't touched her coffee; he was on his second cup.

"Maybe I thought after Ben, if I gave you up, if I was a good girl, if I played by the rules, I'd be protected."

"There are no rules. There is no way to protect yourself. Life is a crap shoot. You win some. You lose some. You do the best you can. You deal with what comes along. If you survive, you get stronger."

"Maybe you're right. All I know is that I was trying to be the senator's good daughter and take happy pictures of people. Then I took that picture and all hell broke loose again. Before they caught Trevor and saved that little boy, his mother called me. She said my picture made her son's loss so much more real than it had been before. She made me feel so guilty and sad…and bad…just like I'd felt when Ben died. And again there was nothing I could do."

"There never is."

Heather's eyes pooled with tears. "She…she said that if

her child died, she would never get that last picture of him
alive out of her mind. That she had thousands of calls about
sightings, that I put her in hell by making that crime so
public and so personal—''

''Oh, baby, baby— But one of those calls because of
your picture made it possible for the cops to find her kid.''

''I can't go through it again, knowing I'm to blame if
anything happens to Nicky.''

''I knew you stopped taking pictures— Honey, life is
always a gamble. You can't blame yourself every time
something goes wrong. Nicky's going to be okay.''

''If I hadn't taken that picture—''

''That child would have died. *Because* of you the biggest
manhunt of the century was a success. You were a hero.''

''My own child's in danger now. Trevor wrote me from
prison. He sort of loves me in some twisted way. He told
me all about his childhood. He told me his father took him
away, and his mother never tried to find him. He told me
how scared he'd been of his daddy. How lost he'd felt away
from his mother. I never wrote back. His letters got angrier
and angrier—''

''Heather,'' he rasped. ''Stop torturing yourself.''

''Just…just hold me.''

''I should've realized what you went through.'' He'd
been too jealous of her other boyfriends. He should have
asked about the Pulitzer.

Joey wanted to fold her closer, to caress her silken hair,
her smooth throat.

She had not come to him for that. He swallowed hard
and fought to regain control. Still, he had to lay out the
new conditions of their marriage now, or he might never
have the courage to do so.

''Heather, before you came back down here, I was thinking…about us. About what you said in the plane and then
later, upstairs. About what I put you and your family
through. I—I was wrong…to force you to marry me. You

need to make your own choices. Not your father's. Not mine, either.''

What little color remained in her cheeks drained away. When she stared up at him with glazed eyes, he realized this was the worst time in the world to be sorting out their problems.

''I shouldn't lay this on you now, but you were right, and I was wrong,'' he said.

Her beautiful face was ashen. She couldn't take much more, he thought. He had to get this over fast.

''I'll stay with you,'' he stumbled on blindly, ''through this Trevor thing…. Then I'll let you go.''

''What?''

''You did say you wanted me to stay till—''

Her huge, unseeing eyes clung to his. ''Till we see this through,'' she breathed.

Her tearful silence tore him apart.

''I'm sorry I forced you to marry me,'' he said quietly.

His hand was entangled in her hair. The lamplight on the nearby tables lit her pale face and yellow curls. How easily he could draw her closer. He fought not to remember how her lips had burned him that night in his cabin.

Her face was as quiet as death. He wanted to touch her. To hold her. To keep her safe. To know what she was thinking and feeling. But no matter how much he needed answers or for her to share his deepest feelings, he couldn't force them.

''So, we'll go home,'' he said. ''We won't tell anybody we're getting a divorce. Till Trevor's caught.''

''Divorce?'' she squeaked. The heartbeat in her throat stilled.

''I won't leave till I know you're safe,'' he persisted blindly.

She drew a deep breath. ''Whatever you say, Joey.''

Her bleak gaze and the finality in her tone killed something inside him. He drew her closer, and she began to sob.

Ten

Heather was gorgeous in a simple white gown set off by stunning silver jewelry. Although Joey pretended indifference, her amethyst eyes dominated her face and *his* soul.

They walked up the stairs separately, not talking, not touching. Nicky dawdled behind them, proudly showing off the new car Joey had bought him to Louie.

"I wanted a gun, but Dad bought me this," Nicky shrieked.

Heather turned. "I'm sorry to put you through this, Joey."

He rang the bell. "I'm okay."

"Daddy's so jealous—"

"He used to hate me because I was a nobody. Now he hates me because I'm a somebody."

"Mostly he hates you for marrying me."

"He's a difficult man."

"Lighten up on him...tonight...please."

Joey's mouth thinned. As always, she defended her father.

"This last month hasn't been easy...for any of us," she said.

"Tell me about it." He saw her fright and softened his tone. "With any luck, it won't last forever. The cops'll get Trevor. And you'll all be happily rid of me. You'll be safe again. You can go back to being Daddy's good little girl."

She whitened. Her violet eyes grew huge in the shadows. "It was always more fun being bad with you."

"Where the hell's your mother?" He jammed his fist on the doorbell again.

When she heard Nellie, Heather slid her hand into his. Unwanted electricity ripped through him. He stiffened.

She was smiling adoringly up at him when Nellie and Julia opened the door. Heather squeezed his fingers and winked flirtatiously, and he hated the hot bolt that raced through him.

He was too damn easy. Every day he craved more of her. Every day, she gave him less.

The heat of her fingers against Joey's skin became unbearable. He wanted to tear his hand free, to run. He stood his ground.

Dear God. Playing her newlywed lover in public when she couldn't stand him was sheer torture.

"There you are, my darlings. I'm afraid I'm running a little late," Nellie said, her smile brightening at the sight of her daughter's flushed face. "I'm sure you lovebirds can entertain yourselves a minute or two while Julia and I tend to a few last-minute details—"

After the usual, breezy hugs, Nellie scurried back to her kitchen and Julia, who'd miraculously made herself indispensable to the Wades during this tense time, ran into the dining room.

Heather's pretty smile froze. She pulled her hand free of his.

He steeled himself not to look at her, not to crave affection when they were alone. Out of the corner of his eye, he was aware of her watching him as he moved away from her to the window.

"I know you don't like these Sunday evenings with my family," she said.

"I know you don't like acting like we have a real marriage," he replied.

"Oh, Joey, do you think they'll ever catch him?"

"Not soon enough." He scanned the line of trees fringing the fence as well as the thick growth along the creek.

"How long will we have to endure all the reporters and the cops camped at the ranch gates and swarming all over town?"

"You mean how long do you have to endure…me?"

She chewed her bottom lip. "Every time we go out, they're all over us."

"I don't like it any better than you do."

"Thank you for staying. I—I've never been so scared in my whole life."

"I'm not sure I've been much help. My fame is why Trevor's after Nicky, and your life's such a circus."

"It's made me understand what you have to put up with, though."

"As if you care."

She drew a deep breath. "Do you have to make those constant biting remarks?"

"Sorry."

He lapsed into an awkward silence. Suddenly the house seemed smaller, homier—worse. He could hear Nellie bustling about clanking pots and pans. Nicky was making car sounds as he sent toy cars flying across the porch. Travis was sulking in his study. Julia was setting the table with china and silver.

Almost, his marriage felt real. Maybe that was why Joey had come to hate these ritual Sunday dinners. And what had she meant on the porch, saying it was more fun to be bad with him?

Maybe marriage was easy for some men.

But it was hard for Joey.

When he'd walked down the aisle, he'd wanted Heather and Nicky more than anything. But he hadn't bargained on living in an armed encampment alongside a father-in-law who detested him, or trying to protect Nicky and Heather from a madman. He hadn't considered how a month of cops and reporters and fans and Trevor would terrify and estrange his wife. If he'd hoped to win Heather by staying, he'd made no progress. They were further apart than ever.

Joey frowned when Travis stomped into the living room carrying a couple of newspapers. He stooped to hug Heather.

"Hello," Joey said.

With a cold shrug, Travis stalked past him. Belligerently he slapped two newspapers onto the elaborately set table in front of Julia.

"Every damn word's about your brother again! He gets the headlines and they bury me inside the articles. I'm the senator. He's just a trashy pop star."

"You two aren't in competition, Mr. Wade," Julia said.

"It's easy for you to take that saintly view, young woman! He took *my* daughter by force."

Joey watched Heather follow her father into the dining room and sink obediently into a tall chair beside Julia.

Bold, inch-high letters screamed, Kidnapper on the Rampage. Maniac Stalks Joey Fasano's Secret Lovechild.

There were pictures of Joey in the arms of the aggressive blonde who'd waylaid him beside the elevators in Vegas.

"The media gets more hostile every day," Travis said. "They're determined to ruin me."

"You aren't even mentioned," Nellie said.

Travis turned purple. "A fact Fasano and you never let me forget."

Heather went rigid. The slender lines of her back were even straighter than her chair.

"The main thing is Nicky's safety," Joey said in a taut, low tone as he sat down beside her.

Heather and Julia paled. Startled, they looked away from the newspapers' headlines, from each other, from both men, out the windows to Nicky who was making his toy car zoom along the railing. Julia clasped Heather's hand reassuringly.

"He's okay, dear."

Not for the first time, Joey envied the two women's friendship. He marveled that his sister adored the boy as much as Heather. Julia had insisted on coming to stay as soon as she'd heard Nicky was in danger. Things had been tense between the Wades and Julia, but Julia's sweet temperament and willingness to help had quickly won them over. Although Joey loved Julia, he was almost jealous of her closeness to his wife, and of her new easiness with his in-laws.

"They'll get Pilot," Nellie said cheerily in an effort to defuse the tension of her little family dinner party. "Then we can get back to our lives."

"But will I win my election?" Travis thundered. "The damn media's forgotten me. Will they start concentrating on important issues like that national water bill I introduced?"

Nellie's diamonds flashed as she lifted his newspapers off the table to make room for a heaping bowl of potatoes au gratin. "Travis, if you insist on buying these horrible newspapers, would you please read them in your study? And you upset everybody by carrying on and on about your election."

"Me?" her father roared indignantly. "I'm not the villain here." He glared at Joey. "The damn criminal's after Nicky because of *him*."

"This situation is difficult for us all," Nellie said mildly.

"I'm sick of living in this armed camp. Sick of all of you blaming me instead of—" Again he stared pointedly at Joey.

"Julia," Nellie began. "Would you please say grace?"

When Julia finished saying a prayer in which she said they should all be thankful for having each other during this time of crisis, everybody fell silent and stared at the food and each other awkwardly for a long moment. Then Nellie handed Travis a carving knife and told him to slice the roast.

Each Sunday dinner was more tense than the last. Not that Joey didn't make a huge effort to be polite, but Travis's hostility made genuine friendship impossible. It hurt that Heather always sided with her father.

With a fierce glance toward Joey, Travis hacked huge chunks off the pink roast with Nellie's big silver knife.

"Remember what I told you about reasonable portions, dear," Nellie whispered from her end of the table.

Eyeing Joey again, Travis's knife flashed above the roast, and another slab of meat collapsed like a boulder into oozing juices.

"I think…that's enough meat," Nellie said.

"This is my house, and I'm carving my way," Travis said stonily as he continued to stare at Joey while he hacked at the meat as if he were contemplating murder.

"Yes, dear."

Everyone ate the ragged bits of meat in silence. When they were done they did not linger for coffee and conversation. Instead they fled to opposite ends of the house. Heather and Julia joined Nicky outside. Joey went to the den to read. Only when he went to the bookcase, he saw Heather's photo albums under a chair. Instead of a completed album, he grabbed a box of pictures. He sat down in the senator's big leather chair and peeled back the brown, cardboard flaps.

He flipped through a few snapshots of Ben and Julia

without really looking at them. Then there were several of
Julia looking plumper than usual. Ben was touching her
stomach. In another Ben was kneeling, his smiling face
pressed against her thickening middle.

Dimly Joey heard the little car fly into the wall. Nicky
burst into laughter. So did Julia.

There were more pictures of Julia near a Louisiana
bayou. She was fatter than ever now.

Why was her young face so slim, her cheeks so hollow?

Joey's hand began to shake. In every successive picture
without Ben, Julia's eyes were sad and lost while her girth
expanded.

She hadn't been fat.

Heather's laughter joined Julia's.

Slowly, Joey turned and saw Julia's dark head bent over
the little red car Nicky held in his palm.

Joey shook his head, not wanting to believe. Then he
studied the picture of his sister, again noting her thin face,
her matchstick arms, her slender legs, her cute pot belly
under the maternity blouse.

He stared at the window again. Behind Julia's glowing
face, the sky was opalescent. The moon was coming up as
the sun was going down. Slim-waisted, laughing, Julia was
as rare and exquisite as the beautiful evening.

Ben had died. His sister had run away.

There is no baby.

Heather had told the truth.

For one month he'd believed Nicky was his.

For one wonderful, terrible month.

He shouldn't have married Heather. She'd had her father's interests at heart. Never his. He wouldn't have married her, if she'd told him the truth.

Maybe Trevor never would have broken out and come
after them.

Their marriage, this past month, Trevor stalking Nicky—
it was all a horrible, avoidable mistake.

If only Julia had told him—

If only Heather had—

Instead they'd conspired against him and condemned him to hell.

Nicky was racing down to the creek to float a paper boat Joey had made him.

Wordlessly Heather plucked the extraordinary photograph of a pregnant Julia out of Joey's brown hand.

She blushed as she stared at the grainy picture.

"Why didn't you tell me?" he whispered.

She bit her lip.

"I'm glad you know the truth," Julia said, coming between them. "Nicky's mine. And Ben's. But only biologically."

"Why?" Joey asked.

"Heather was heartbroken when she lost Ben and your baby...and you."

"Leave me out of it, damn it."

"Joey, she loved Nicky from the first. I couldn't take care of him. I could barely go on...after Ben died. I found Heather living in Louisiana with her grandmother. I practically collapsed on their doorstep. You know how Daddy was about sex and my virginity. Ben was going to marry me. When he died, I had to run away. I had to be as pure as snow. And I wanted to be that way, too. I loved Ben so much, but when he died... I couldn't tell anybody back home. Not even you, Joey. I—I thought God was punishing me—"

Joey stared from his sister to the little boy bending over the rushing water. "He thinks I'm his real dad."

"You are...now."

"No."

Wild panic flashed in Heather's eyes he whirled on her. "Why didn't you tell me?"

"I didn't think you'd understand. It's hard to explain

why I do the crazy things I do. Mother and Daddy never understand.''

''I'm not them.''

''Julia was so fragile. I fell in love with Nicky instantly.''

''I would have loved him too.''

''He was Ben's. It was like I had something of Ben again. And so did my parents. But then, even from the first, Joey, Nicky was like you.''

''Don't play me!''

''I wanted him. I loved him. Every day, he became more like you.''

''Don't.''

''I was upset.''

''Somehow you survived.''

When Heather reached toward him, he recoiled.

''I wanted you out of my life. I couldn't tell you about him.''

''Why did you let me believe this entire past month he was mine?''

''I did try once.''

''No. You used me. You were afraid of Trevor. You played on my emotions.''

''You forced me—''

''If you'd told me the truth, I wouldn't have. I want a divorce. The sooner, the better.''

Without another word, he strode past her toward his truck.

Nicky saw him and ran to him. ''Daddy, the boat sank!''

''Later, Tiger.''

Joey hurled himself into the cab.

''Take me with you, Dad—''

''Go to your mother.''

Moonlight glinted off Joey's whiskey bottle. Joey's chest ached as he studied two old photographs of Heather. She'd been eight and in pigtails. He held the picture so close tha her freckled face loomed huge. Enlarged, her childish features became hideous, devouring him.

He let it flutter through his fingers to the floor.

Where had he ever fitted into her life? Her family hadn't wanted him. She'd been ashamed of him. He'd forced her to marry him. She didn't want to be married to a wild, bad movie star whose fame diminished her egotistical father and made her life crazy and unsafe. She'd only let him stay because she was afraid of Trevor.

He had thought he could bear it—living with her in the same house, pretending he was her husband, learning to love *his* son while he protected them and tried to find that bastard Trevor Pilot.

His son?

Surely he could go on pretending. He was, after all, an actor.

Yet every moment, every hour he'd spent with them, had etched deeper grooves into his heart. Even though he'd lost his temper this afternoon, his feelings for her and Nicky were so intense they scared the hell out of him. He was a man obsessed. Not a day went by that he didn't remember how Heather had quivered beneath him in ecstasy. Not a night went by that he didn't want her.

What difference did it make whose kid Nicky was? Or if she'd lied? There were more profound truths and needs at stake.

Joey took a long pull from the bottle. His head was muddled with whiskey, but nothing seemed to stop the pain as he sat hunched over Heather's boxes of pictures in his living room.

He'd driven for hours. He hadn't come home till the sky was black and moon high, and he was sure she and Nicky would be asleep. Then he'd grabbed a bottle and sifted through old pictures.

As a kid Heather had photographed every bug she saw, every tree, every pet, everything Julia and Ben and he had

done together. There was even a picture of his mongrel
eating a cherry cobbler Nellie had set in a window to cool.
A picture of Joey buried in piles of leaves, another of him
showing off by hanging upside down from a tree. There
were pictures of Ben and Julia kissing in the backseat of
Ben's sports car. Ben, who'd been a reckless driver, had
chased them for a mile trying to get that roll of film.

There had been so much love.

And so much pain.

In the last picture of Ben and Julia together, Ben was so
alive.

Poor darling Julia. That special glow in her eyes was
gone forever. If Joey lost Heather and Nicky, he would be
plunged into the same black hell.

Even when Joey was so furious at her, he wanted to
strangle her, he'd never stopped lov—

After he'd simmered down tonight, Joey understood why
Heather might have done what she'd done. But her sacrifice
only made him despise himself for not guessing the truth
about his own sister. He'd been so damned self-absorbed,
he hadn't worried enough about Julia.

Instead, he'd resented her for vanishing.

Joey pitched Ben's smiling picture into the box and stood
up.

His head throbbed from the whiskey. Somehow he had
to drag himself to bed, to try to get through another night
knowing Heather was in the next bedroom. He stumbled
toward the hall, only to stop in midstride when he heard
muted sobs behind her door.

Gut instinct told him to stalk past her room.

Instead he turned her doorknob. "Heather—"

Her crying ceased abruptly. He pushed the door wider.

The silvery sheet molded the outlines of her voluptuous
body. A lump constricted his throat.

"Are you all right?" he whispered, his voice hoarse.

"I'm so sorry I didn't tell you before—"

He froze. "It's okay." Then he crossed the room and sank down beside her.

Her luxuriant golden hair was spread across her pillow. He wanted to touch it, to run his hands through it.

Slowly Joey pulled her into his arms. She smelled of soap and perfume as she nuzzled against him. Her cotton nightgown was cool and yet damp, her satin skin as warm as Texas sunlight. Just holding her after not really touching her for a whole month ignited soul-deep longings as well as those low carnal impulses he had to fight so hard to suppress.

Her breathing quickened. His own became quick and raspy. When he tried to push her away, she foolishly clung.

Her soft breasts pressed his chest. He knew the exact moment when her nipples hardened, when her skin heated and lit his body with desire.

"Nicky went to bed in tears."

"I'll talk to him tomorrow."

"Joey, I'm sorry I didn't tell you about Nicky. But I— I've never told anyone. I guess I got used to keeping him a secret to protect Julia. She was so desperate after he was born. When I used to carry him to her, she would stare into space and tell me to feed him or to hold him. They grew apart. I became his mother. It just happened."

"I'm glad you were there for them...even if I wasn't."

"Julia started going to church. By the time she knew her life belonged to God, Nicky belonged to me. Maybe you could become his father the same—"

"No—" Joey closed his eyes and clenched his hands.

"Don't go," she pleaded. Her velvet tone was laced with need.

"I don't want to start anything I can't finish."

Her long dark lashes veiled her eyes in shadow. Never had she looked more vulnerable or more feminine. Her hands wound seductively around his neck. The liquor weakened him, causing his senses to reel when she snuggled closer.

Then her mouth touched his, and the honeyed, familiar taste of her soft lips and the opulent warmth of her body made him jump back.

She was Heather. The brat he had teased. The woman he worshipped and longed for. His wife.

In name only.

She hadn't wanted to marry him.

With unsteady hands, he gently pushed her away. Her fingers clutched at his shoulders and then at his arms.

"Come back to me," she begged. But he ripped himself free and went to his own room.

As if burned into his brain, he saw the swell of her breasts and the dark circles of her nipples beading her thin cotton nightgown.

Her whisper haunted him. *Come back to me.*

He counted and recounted the ceiling tiles, but her image burned and her sultry voice sang like a siren's.

His nerves were wound so tight, he couldn't sleep. So, he got up and went outside, scanning the trees for any danger.

He wanted out of this marriage.

The sooner the better.

The band began. Heather risked an adoring glance at Joey when he started.

He hated her. Even though he stood beside her, tapping his foot to the heavy beat, he rarely looked at her. Not once had he asked her to dance. She lowered her gaze to his long shadow. Joined to hers, the dark shapes flowed to the very edge of the terraces where dozens of couples whirled.

Did any of their guests suspect that her heart was breaking?

"Do you see him?" Joey demanded in that cold, estranged tone that cut her.

Ever since he'd discovered Nicky wasn't his, ever since he'd kissed her in her moonlit bedroom, his black gaze had been glacial. Never did he smile or touch her.

Nicky was why he'd married her. Every day, Joey grew icier. Nicky knew something was wrong and was terrified.

"Is Daddy mad at me?"

"It's my fault."

"How come he has his own room? I thought married people slept together?"

She had not known how to answer.

"Well?" Joey's harsh voice jerked Heather back to the party. "Do you see Trevor?"

Tonight the ranch gates and fences were only spottily guarded. Thus, Heather's eyes grew frightened as she scanned the white party tents set up on the lawns that sloped down to the rushing creek and then the faces of their guests and plainclothesmen for that one diabolical face.

She shook her head.

"Stare harder. Look at everyone. He might have done something to change his appearance."

"I'd *feel* him."

"Keep looking."

"I have. Dozens of times." Blinded by tears, she turned. "Oh, Joey, why…why a party? Why now? When…when we're so unhappy?"

"If we want this farce over, we have to force his hand."

"I'm scared."

"It'll be worse if he doesn't show up."

"You don't understand. I'm afraid of what's happening to us."

"No wonder," Joey said bitterly. "If my gamble doesn't work, we could be stuck with each other for years."

Stuck with each other.

"Is that how you feel?"

"Don't tell me you're happy," he replied sarcastically. "You've lost weight. You don't sleep."

Didn't he have eyes? A heart? Couldn't he see she loved him? That all the mistakes she'd made had stemmed from the one mistake of trying to deny who she was and what he meant to her?

True, her father opposed her marriage. But she had decided to live her own life.

Joey was the man she loved. He was a good man. She hated hurting her father, but Nicky loved Joey. Nicky introduced Joey to everyone as his dad, his famous movie star dad.

"He's my real dad. He plays football! And he knows karate!"

Stuck with each other.

Joey wanted to end their marriage and resume his glamorous life.

Suddenly Heather couldn't stand beside Joey and play his game. Choosing the path that wound down to the boathouse, she ran from the terrace. From the boathouse she stared at the dark, rushing water. Here Larry had tried to seduce her.

Here Joey had saved her.

What if he hadn't come?

The black water and dark cypress trees swam in a blur of tears. She picked up a rock to throw it into the creek. When her stone splashed into the black depths Joey's image floated on top the foamy bubbles as if to mock her.

"Go away, damn you—" she wept.

She picked up another rock. But when she pulled back her hand to fling it after the first, a warm fist closed around hers in a viselike grip.

Joey was there. She'd seen his reflection.

Still, she screamed.

"It's just me, babe."

"Joey—"

His hand gentled. "How come you ran?"

She fought to make her manner light and offhand, but a shudder of pain went through her. "No reason."

His gaze fixed hers.

He saw. He knew.

"Baby." Very slowly his arms closed tenderly around her.

She forgot the pain and the awful frustration of the past month and let herself be drawn to him.

"I was afraid maybe you'd seen him," Joey said, "and gotten scared."

"It's not that." Her voice was choked. "I'm fine."

"*Fine?* My favorite word." He brushed his hand through her golden hair, winding the silken strands around his fingers.

Her father was frowning at her. So what. Her father had married the woman he loved. He'd have to understand.

She swallowed and turned to Joey.

The music was strangely haunting. Or maybe it was just Joey. Like a dreamer, she felt herself in a strange, new land. In real life she was forbidden to be held or touched by him. In her dream, she was freer, lighter. There were no rules.

Beyond, she could hear music and their guests laughing. In the distance Nicky shrieked. Only dimly was she aware of lights flickering beneath the tents, of the wind murmuring above in the tall cypress trees, that seemed magically to grow so tall they reached the stars. Like a dreamer in some enchanted land, she held her fairy tale lover in her arms.

Love. Strange, how in her dream she wasn't afraid to confess her true feelings.

"I love you," she whispered.

He smiled, pulling her tighter, as if the word no longer ate at him like acid.

"Don't leave me," she begged, her heart in her eyes.

"No way."

Strange, how in her dream all she wanted was for him to hold her forever.

He held her, caressing her, and when she lifted her mouth toward his, he seemed not to have the slightest inclination to resist.

"Dance with me," she invited with a dazzling smile.

Her body flowed into his. They began to move together, becoming one. He fused his mouth to hers.

"Heather. Oh, God, Heather."

Like dreamers in their own magic world, they danced to a slow, erotic melody only they heard.

He kissed her. She wanted to run away with him, to be swept tighter and tighter into his arms.

Deep inside herself she knew the dream would end and he would break her heart.

For now his kissing her, his holding her, was enough.

Sensing that he was powerfully enchanted too, she began to laugh. She tossed her head back as they danced, and her face became incandescent. His laughter joined hers. People turned to watch them.

Joey pulled her closer, lifting her higher and higher into his arms. Round and round, they swirled. She clung long after the music stopped.

His kiss deepened.

Heat consumed her.

"I love you," she whispered.

He kissed her mouth and then her face, her ears, and her throat.

Her fingertips slid under his long hair, around his neck, cupped his face. "Do you realize," she said breathlessly, "that you let me say I love you?"

"You are my wife. You should be able to say whatever you like."

"Ours has not been the usual sort of marriage."

"Maybe we should change the rules."

"Will you say you love me then?"

"On a night like this, anything's possible."

"Oh, Joey, my darling—"

When he picked her up to carry her deeper into the woods, his grip was both savage and tender. She held him with equal intensity.

They had forgotten Trevor Pilot.

Joey had carried her to the edge of the black woods, when a scream, followed by an explosion shocked them back to reality.

Joey's arms fell away. He backed away from her. White-faced, his blank stare was that of a sleeper awakened from a pleasant dream he couldn't quite remember.

The cypress trees shrank to their normal size.

Nicky's running footsteps sent pebbles pinging into her ankles.

"Daddy, a big guy grabbed me! Louie grabbed him! A cop shot the bad guy! Come see! There's...blood... and...and—"

Her father yelled her name.

Heather scooped Nicky up and ran toward the gathering crowd.

Trevor was rolling on the ground in a pool of blood like a mad dog. When he saw her, he spit at her. "I'll get you—"

"Joey!" she screamed, clutching Nicky tighter as she stared into the crowd.

A burly cop leaned down and cuffed Trevor, who was sobbing now.

"This isn't my fault. Nobody ever loved me. You didn't write back—"

The cops led Trevor Pilot away.

"Joey!" Heather whispered. "Joey—"

Nellie and Travis embraced her.

"Where's Joey?" Heather wept.

"Gone," her father said. "It's just as well."

"No!"

"We love you," her parents said. "Everything's all right. You're safe. Our lives can get back to normal."

"Not without Joey."

"You love Fasano's hellraising brat that much?" her father demanded incredulously.

"I do. Oh, Daddy, I'm sorry if that makes you unhappy, but I really really do."

"Then why the hell did he leave you?" Travis demanded grumpily.

Reporters swarmed toward the famous senator and his daughter. They shoved microphones in Heather's face.

"Will they lock Pilot up for good?"

"Daddy, would you talk to them?" Heather pleaded.

"Mom!" Nicky shrieked, wiggling to get down. "Could I see the cop's gun?"

She clutched Nicky tighter and pushed through the reporters. Travis smiled as they swelled around him. He swung an arm around his wife. Senator Wade was in his element. His chest swelled with newfound pride under the media barrage. "The party tonight was a trap to catch Pilot. It was all my idea. You see—"

Holding tight to Nicky, whose bright gaze was fixed on the cop's holster, Heather wandered away as her father expounded on his own heroism.

Another night she might have listened and laughed. Tonight all she could think of was Joey.

The month of pretense was over.

So was their marriage.

She'd lost him forever.

Eleven

Joey ripped hangers and clothes out of his closet and tossed them onto the bed in a tangle of coatsleeves and trouser legs. In the distance he could hear the band resume its playing at his father-in-law's party.

The front door banged shut.

"Dad! Dad! I got to touch a gun! A real one!"

Nicky raced excitedly into the bedroom and then froze.

"Dad? What are you doing? You're making a big mess."

Joey grabbed a drawer and shook its contents on top of the tumble of jackets and trousers. He then shook out a second drawer and stuffed the whole mess into a garbage bag.

"Aren't you supposed to fold stuff and put it in the suitcase?"

"Who told you that?"

"Mommy."

"Women will complicate the hell out of your life...if you let them. Which is something I don't ever intend to do again."

Joey slung the bag over his wide shoulder and strode toward the door with a show of masterful indifference.

Nicky's soft, pleading voice stopped him dead in his tracks. "Dad, don't go."

"I have to."

"Why?"

"'Cause I promised your mother."

No need to explain how he felt when Trevor had been captured. Heather's parents had embraced *her*. She'd embraced Nicky. She didn't need him anymore. Maybe she never had.

"She wants you to stay," Joey said.

"She has a funny way of showing it."

"Don't you love me?"

There it was—the *love* word. Joey ignored the way it ripped his heart.

"This isn't about you."

"But I thought...you were my dad—"

Joey knelt down to Nicky's level. He met the little boy's dazed, black gaze. "I am."

"I've been waiting my whole life for my real dad."

Joey sucked in a deep breath. "Someday you'll understand."

"Grandpa said you'd rather be a movie star than my dad!"

"That's not true."

Nicky pivoted. "If you go it is."

"Nicky— Son—"

"You made Mom cry!" Nicky dashed past Joey's outstretched arms and raced out of the room. "You're making me cry."

The walls closed around Joey. What was he going to do without Nicky? Without Heather? He remembered his father's beatings, his dread of going home as a kid. He remembered the lonely nights in L.A. For a few brief, shining weeks, he'd almost been part of a real family.

They didn't want him.

Suddenly lifetime of public, meaningless relationships with fame-crazed starlets stretched before him. For all its glitter, his future loomed bleak and empty—hopeless.

"Damn."

Heather was sprawled across her bed. She felt a squeezing sensation in her chest as she devoured a tabloid story about Joey escorting a pretty starlet to a film premiere. Beside the magazine was a thick manila envelope stuffed with legal documents Joey's lawyer had sent. A newspaper lay open to a feature on Trevor's troubled childhood.

Nellie pushed the door open. "Why do you torture yourself?"

Heather's gaze remained fixed on the beautiful brunette in Joey's arms. "Because I can't resist pictures…of him. These pictures…and Julia's calls are all I have to tell me how he is."

"He loves you, Heather."

Heather patted the manila envelope. "Then why did he send me divorce papers?"

"He married you."

"Because of Nicky."

"He's wanted you since the day you were born. Your father and I…we thought he was like his father. But he isn't. Fame ruins a lot of people, but Joey has too much character. Some women would think they were lucky to have a man as extraordinary as the one you're throwing away—"

"Mother, *he* left."

"You let him."

"He didn't even say goodbye. It's over."

"Not in this lifetime. I watched you two together. His feelings were in his eyes every time he looked at you...and Nicky."

"You're wrong!"

"What if I'm right? What if you're both too stubborn and too afraid of being hurt to even talk?"

"Mother, please—"

"Look. I'm the reason your father hates Joey. I...I never told you this. Your father didn't want me to. But I was Deo's girl before I met your father. Your dad was jealous of Deo and, therefore, of Joey who looked so much like him."

"What?"

"When you got pregnant, your father blamed me. He said the weakness for Fasanos came from me. Deo dated me because everybody knew I was a virgin, and he had a thing about virgins. When I left him, he told everybody he'd taken my virginity. Your father and he had a terrible fight. I understand why Julia couldn't tell her father about Ben...or Nicky. Surely Joey does, too. I'm sure he understands why you did what you did."

"He doesn't."

"This...this whole mess is my fault. Deo was wrong for me. I didn't like you dating his son because it always made your father mad at me. Your father thinks money and position are everything. Joey was poor. We thought someone like Larry could give you more than Joey."

"And now—"

"I imagine that without love life can seem pretty hollow."

Heather met her mother's gaze. "Thank you for caring

enough to tell me these things, but I have to work this out on my own.''

''Call him.''

''You can't tell me what to do any more—''

The phone rang.

Hoping it was Joey, Heather leapt on it.

Julia's voice said, ''Joey's miserable.''

''He served me with divorce papers today.''

''Burn them.''

''He wants out, Julia.''

''Did I tell you he was offered a really serious part? The kind of meaty role he's wanted to play for years. He…he won't take it.''

''Why?''

''Maybe for the same reason you aren't going to sign those papers. His heart's not in it.''

''Julia—''

''He can't concentrate. He can't work. Oh, he tries. But he can't get over you.''

''I don't want to talk about him.''

''He doesn't want to talk about you, either,'' Julia said. ''Why'd he leave?''

''Because his heart was breaking,'' Julia said. ''Because he loves you too much. You hurt him. We both did. Remember how all four of us always played together as kids? Then Ben died. You and I went away together. We had Nicky. We left him out…all those years. How would you feel?''

After Julia's call, Heather moodily read the divorce papers. Even though the settlement was generous, the language was so cold, so final.

With a leaden heart she moved listlessly about her parents' ranch house. If she wasn't going to be Joey's wife, she was going to have to get a job, move on.

Several editors had called because of all the recent publicity, asking her to return to her career. She had been playing with her camera lately. Maybe she would.

But the only thing she wanted, the only thing she had ever really wanted, was Joey. Without him, an important piece of herself would always be missing.

"You can't say no! The part of Sam Rydell is made for you." Mac's impatient voice broke up in a burst of static.

"Can't hear you."

"Titania said for you to call your wife."

"I don't need a marriage counselor!"

"Hey, you sound hot, really hot. Why don't you cool off? Go for a swim in that kidney-shaped pool of yours. Who knows? Maybe you'll find a naked mermaid."

"God forbid."

"Hey! Okay. Confession time." Mac's voice had a strange, crisp edge. "What if I told you I gave a very beautiful woman the key to your garage and poolhouse? Hey! I just dropped her off. She doesn't have a swimsuit. She's stripping as we speak—"

"You'd better be lying, or I'll hunt you down and strangle you with my bare hands."

"Happy birthday, lover— Put those hands of yours and that overabundant passion to…er…X-rated uses."

"It's not my birthday," Joey yelled.

"Gotcha a prez anyway."

"Have you lost your mind?"

The line crackled and went dead.

When he tried Mac's cell phone, Titania picked up.

"Chill out, Joey, in your pool," she purred through light static.

"Get Mac."

"You've got company, superstud." Then she hung up, too.

Fury drove Joey to the long windows that looked out on his pool. He ripped the cord. Draperies swirled open. Silver light glimmered across the dark surface of his pool.

A wavelet slapped over the edge of his swimming pool. A second wave splashed over the tile lip, spreading glimmer all the way to his lawn.

What the hell? He stared as more wet glimmer painted his terrace. Either the moonlight was playing tricks or the smooth, alabaster shape of a woman was cutting through the water.

At least she could swim.

Were those lovely arms lifting and falling, slicing the shadowy waters? Were those really shapely, bare feet flutter-kicking, sending ripples across the smooth water?

Joey inhaled a harsh breath.

Who the hell was she?

Call the cops.

There was something so damnably familiar about that slim form.

Moonlight shone on a long, frizzled tail of trailing wet hair. At the bright yellow ringlets, a dull knife-twist of pain stabbed his heart.

Heather.

Don't go out. Buzz Louie.

Warm, salty air blew against him as he raced outside down his coiled, metal staircase.

The woman swam toward the shallow end. He reached the tiled steps when she did.

She placed a slim, wet hand on the blue-painted tile step beneath his black boot and slanted violet eyes up at him. Long lashes batted flirtily, seducing him.

"This is one helluva hideout," she whispered huskily.

Her endearing smile was bold and impish and too sexy for words. "I thought you'd never invite me to see it. Want to show me what you've got?"

"Heather—"

"Why don't you get naked?" she coaxed.

"Louie—"

"Gone—"

"What?"

"I gave him the night off."

"You have no authority—"

"I'm your wife, remember?"

"We're divorced."

"Not just yet."

"I sent you papers."

"I used them to light a fire. Nicky and I cooked marshmallows."

"I'll send more."

"Be a good boy, and save those trees."

"Heather, what the hell do you think you're doing here?"

"Throwing myself at you. The way all those wild, wicked women in those tabloids do—"

"You're not like them," he whispered huskily, kneeling, folding her small wet hand into his.

"Maybe I want to be. Are you going to pull me out of the pool and kiss me the way you did Daniella?"

"You're not drowning."

"Not yet." She sank under the water. When her bubbles stopped, he frowned.

"Damn it, Heather."

He held his breath till his lungs felt like they'd burst. She didn't come up. Just as he was about to jump in, she sprang up, gulped in air, grabbed his brown wrist, placed her foot against the side of the pool, arched, and lunged backward, yanking him down, down.

"Heather!"

With a huge geyser-like splash, he fell on top of her and gulped in water.

Chlorine stung his sinuses. She wrapped her legs around his waist and her arms around his neck. He snorted and spat water.

"There'd better not be some photographer dangling upside down in a tree," he said, "or we will both be plastered—"

"I hope there is. I'm tired of all those other women staring at me in the grocery store. I want everybody to know you're mine."

"What about your daddy?"

"He'll have to put his spin doctors to work."

"It's about time."

"You taught me that life's a gamble. You have to take risks to get what you want."

"You're not afraid my crazy life will hurt you and your father's precious career?"

They were in waist-deep water when she began to strip him. Clumsily her fingers tore at the buttons of his shirt.

Her eyes grew dark even as her body shone in the glow of the moonlight.

"I thought if I gave you up...if I quit taking pictures, I could be safe," she said. "I thought I could be the daughter they wanted, give them the grandson and son-in-law they wanted. But then you came back. So did Trevor. I learned that all I want is to be your wife. Life is no fun without you. I'm willing to risk anything, everything for you."

He was silent for a long moment.

"So would I," he finally whispered. "So would I."

"Maybe we'll appreciate our marriage a thousand times

more because of those years we were blind to what really matters.''

''Which is?''

''I love you,'' she said, finishing the last button. She tugged his clinging, damp shirt off his muscular torso. ''And you love me. Even if you won't say it.''

''I'll say it.''

When she'd unzipped his jeans and pulled off the rest of his clothes, he joined his flesh to hers. It was oddly sensual the way cool water warmed by her skin flowed against his skin. He held her, half floating, like a dreamer in a magic aquatic wonderland.

She was his wildest fantasy.

No.

She was real.

His happiness was real.

She was his. Unforgotten. Unforgettable. Forever his.

''When?'' she asked, her eyes earnest and huge, her voice bleak and yet expectant.

''When what?''

''When are you going to say it?''

''Oh, that.''

''Of course...*that.*''

''I love you, too,'' he said gently, tenderly. ''I always have and I always will.''

''Well, finally. That took you long enough.''

''Yeah. It did.''

She pressed her body against his. Holding each other, they sank below the surface and stayed there, till his lungs were near bursting.

Together they bobbed upward. She came out of the water laughing, hugging him, kissing him. ''That's as close as I ever want to come to drowning.''

''Me too.''

They stood together in that silvery dark, their arms locked around each other.

"Take me to bed," she said.

"I thought you'd never ask."

Later, after that first frantic, hurried time, he opened his eyes to the warmth of her dazzling smile. She was so beautiful, his blood surged.

He slid into her more slowly the second time, prolonging his pleasure and hers. After all, they had the whole night to enjoy one another; they had the rest of their lives.

They were married.

"From the first moment I ever took you to my hideout, I loved you," he said, his voice low and husky. "I never stopped loving you, no matter how much I wanted to. I never will."

"Ditto."

"Say it," he ordered.

"I love you."

"I can't hear those three words enough times."

"I love you. I love you. I love—"

"Stop—" he commanded.

"Well, make up your mind, Fasano."

"Show me," he ordered. "Kiss me."

She laughed and rested her hot cheek against his warm stomach. "Where? Down there?"

"You choose."

She traced a hand through the swirl of his black chest hair. "I think I'll start with your lips and work my way down."

"You're very good at that."

"I intend to get better, because I intend to get a great deal of practice."

"This is sounding better and better."

"Pucker up, lover."

He owed Mac. Big time. Not that he'd ever admit it to that meddlesome know-it-all.

Joey closed his eyes and gave a deep sigh as her warm mouth gently claimed his.

Then her lips moved downward, and he almost sobbed from the pleasure she gave him.

*   *   *   *   *

FORTUNE'S Children™

The Fortune family requests
the honor of your presence at the weddings of

Silhouette Desire's scintillating new miniseries,
featuring the beloved Fortune family
and five of your favorite authors.

The Secretary and the Millionaire
by Leanne Banks (SD #1208, 4/99)

When handsome Jack Fortune asked his dependable assistant to
become his daughter's temporary, live-in nanny, Amanda Corbain
knew almost all her secret wishes had come true. But Amanda
had one final wish before this Cinderella assignment ended....

The Groom's Revenge
by Susan Crosby (SD #1214, 5/99)

Powerful tycoon Gray McGuire was bent on destroying the
Fortune family. Until he met sweet Mollie Shaw. And this sprightly
redhead was about to show him that the best revenge is...
falling in love!

Undercover Groom
by Merline Lovelace (SD #1220, 6/99)

Who was Mason Chandler? Chloe Fortune thought she knew
everything about her groom. But as their wedding day
approached, would his secret past destroy their love?

Available at your favorite retail outlet.

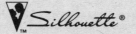

If you enjoyed what you just read,
then we've got an offer you can't resist!

Take 2 bestselling love stories FREE!

Plus get a FREE surprise gift!

Clip this page and mail it to Silhouette Reader Service™

IN U.S.A.
3010 Walden Ave.
P.O. Box 1867
Buffalo, N.Y. 14240-1867

IN CANADA
P.O. Box 609
Fort Erie, Ontario
L2A 5X3

YES! Please send me 2 free Silhouette Desire® novels and my free surprise gift. Then send me 6 brand-new novels every month, which I will receive months before they're available in stores. In the U.S.A., bill me at the bargain price of $3.12 plus 25¢ delivery per book and applicable sales tax, if any*. In Canada, bill me at the bargain price of $3.49 plus 25¢ delivery per book and applicable taxes**. That's the complete price and a savings of over 10% off the cover prices—what a great deal! I understand that accepting the 2 free books and gift places me under no obligation ever to buy any books. I can always return a shipment and cancel at any time. Even if I never buy another book from Silhouette, the 2 free books and gift are mine to keep forever. So why not take us up on our invitation. You'll be glad you did!

225 SEN CNFA
326 SEN CNFC

Name	(PLEASE PRINT)	
Address	Apt.#	
City	State/Prov.	Zip/Postal Code

* Terms and prices subject to change without notice. Sales tax applicable in N.Y.
** Canadian residents will be charged applicable provincial taxes and GST.
   All orders subject to approval. Offer limited to one per household.
   ® are registered trademarks of Harlequin Enterprises Limited.

DES99   ©1998 Harlequin Enterprises Limited

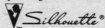

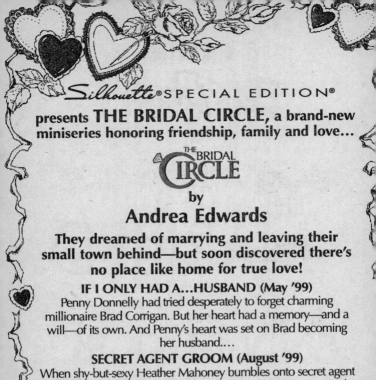

Silhouette® SPECIAL EDITION®

presents **THE BRIDAL CIRCLE,** a brand-new
miniseries honoring friendship, family and love...

THE BRIDAL CIRCLE

by
Andrea Edwards

**They dreamed of marrying and leaving their
small town behind—but soon discovered there's
no place like home for true love!**

IF I ONLY HAD A...HUSBAND (May '99)
Penny Donnelly had tried desperately to forget charming
millionaire Brad Corrigan. But her heart had a memory—and a
will—of its own. And Penny's heart was set on Brad becoming
her husband....

SECRET AGENT GROOM (August '99)
When shy-but-sexy Heather Mahoney bumbles onto secret agent
Alex Waterstone's undercover mission, the only way to protect the
innocent beauty is to claim her as his lady love. Will Heather
carry out her own secret agenda and claim Alex as her groom?

PREGNANT & PRACTICALLY MARRIED
(November '99)
Pregnant Karin Spencer had suddenly lost her memory and
gained a pretend fiancé. Though their match was make-believe,
Jed McCarron was her dream man. Could this bronco-bustin'
cowboy give up his rodeo days for family ways?

Available at your favorite retail outlet.

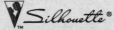

SILHOUETTE® Desire®

M of the A Month N

May '99
LOVE ME TRUE
#1213 by ANN MAJOR

June '99
THE STARDUST COWBOY
#1219 by Anne McAllister

July '99
PRINCE CHARMING'S CHILD
#1225 by Jennifer Greene

August '99
THAT BOSS OF MINE
#1231 by Elizabeth Bevarly

September '99
LEAN, MEAN & LONESOME
#1237 by Annette Broadrick

October '99
FOREVER FLINT
#1243 by Barbara Boswell

MAN OF THE MONTH

For ten years Silhouette Desire
has been giving readers the ultimate in sexy,
irresistible heroes. Come join the celebration as some
of your favorite authors help celebrate our
anniversary with the most sensual, emotional love
stories ever!

Available at your favorite retail outlet.

Silhouette®

Look us up on-line at: http://www.romance.net   SDMOM11

HARLEQUIN *Duets*™

2 new full-length novels by 2 great authors in 1 book for 1 low price!

Buy any Harlequin Duets™ book and **SAVE $1.00!**

SAVE $1.00

when you purchase any

 HARLEQUIN

Duets™ book!

Offer valid May 1, 1999, to October 31, 1999.

Retailer: Harlequin Enterprises Ltd. will pay the face value of this coupon plus 8.0¢ if submitted by the customer for this specified product only. Any other use constitutes fraud. Coupon is nonassignable, void if taxed, prohibited or restricted by law. Consumer must pay any government taxes. Valid in U.S. only. Mail to: Harlequin Enterprises Ltd., P.O. Box 880478, El Paso, TX 88588-0478 U.S.A.

Non NCH customers–for reimbursement submit coupons and proofs of sale directly to: Harlequin Enterprises Ltd., Retail Sales Dept., 225 Duncan Mill Rd., Don Mills (Toronto), Ontario, Canada M3B 3K9.

Printed in Canada 9/98

HDUETC-U

HARLEQUIN® *Makes any time special.*™

Coupon expires October 31, 1999.

5 65373 00051 9   (8100) 1 06254

Look us up on-line at: http://www.romance.net   HDUETC-U

HARLEQUIN *Duets*™

2 new full-length novels by
2 great authors in
1 book for 1 low price!

**Buy any Harlequin Duets™ book
and SAVE $1.00!**

SAVE $1.00

when you purchase any

HARLEQUIN

Duets™ book!

Offer valid May 1, 1999, to October 31, 1999.

HARLEQUIN®
Makes any time special.™

HDUETC-C

**Coupon expires
October 31, 1999.**

52602258

Look us up on-line at: http://www.romance.net   HDUETC-C

SILHOUETTE® *Desire*®

COMING NEXT MONTH

#1219 THE STARDUST COWBOY—Anne McAllister
Man of the Month/Code of the West
Seductive cowboy Riley Stratton claimed he had given up on happily-ever-after, but that didn't stop Dori Malone. When she and her son inherited half the Stratton ranch, she was determined to show Riley that all of his forgotten dreams could come true...but only with her!

#1220 UNDERCOVER GROOM—Merline Lovelace
Fortune's Children: The Brides
Falling in love with her pretend fiancé was not part of Chloe Fortune's plan. But when she found out that he had a secret life, she fled. Now Mason Chandler was out to catch his runaway bride—and convince her that the only place to run was straight into his arms.

#1221 BELOVED SHEIKH—Alexandra Sellers
Sons of the Desert
One moment Zara was about to be kissed by handsome Sheikh Rafi, in the next she was kidnapped! And her captor was a dead ringer for the prince. Whom could she trust? Then "Rafi" appeared with a plan of rescue and a promise to make her queen. Was this a trap...or the only way back into the arms of her beloved sheikh?

#1222 ONE SMALL SECRET—Meagan McKinney
After nine years, Mark Griffin was back in town and playing havoc with Honor Shaw's emotions. Honor had never forgotten the summer she had spent in Mark's arms—and he wanted to pick up where they had left off. But would he still desire her once he learned her secret?

#1223 TAMING TALL, DARK BRANDON—Joan Elliott Pickart
The Bachelor Bet
Confirmed bachelor Brandon Hamilton had long ago given up on the idea of home, hearth and babies. But when he met stubborn beauty Andrea Cunningham, he found himself in danger of being thoroughly and irrevocably tamed....

#1224 THE WILLFUL WIFE—Suzanne Simms
Mathis Hazard didn't want anything to do with Desiree Stratford, but he couldn't turn his back on her need for protection. He agreed to help her as long as she followed *his* rules. But watching over Desiree each day—and night—had Mathis wondering if he was the one in danger...of losing his heart.